EXILES FROM PARADISE

T0343617

Brigitte Adès is a writer, journalist, and the UK Bureau Chief of the foreign affairs journal *Politique Internationale*. She has published in-depth interviews with political and economic leaders such as Margaret Thatcher, Mikhail Gorbachev, David Cameron, Larry Summers and Tony Blair, as well as writers including Graham Greene and Arthur Miller. She also writes for *Le Point*, *Le Figaro* and the *New York Times International Edition*, among other publications.

Brigitte studied international relations at Oxford, where she met a young Iranian student who became her husband. She lives between London and Paris. *Exiles from Paradise* is her first novel.

Iain Watson's translations include books by Victor Segalen and Paul Claudel from the French, and Fernando Pessoa from the Spanish. He speaks French, Spanish, Greek and Italian, and reads Latin fluently. He is the author of several short stories, yet to be published.

Rosie Capell graduated in French from Worcester College, Oxford. She revised the translation of *Exiles from Paradise*. She now works as a full-time translator at franklyfluent agency in London.

EXILES FROM PARADISE

BRIGITTE ADÈS

Translated from the French by
Iain Watson and Rosie Capell

A

Arcadia Books Ltd
139 Highlever Road
London W10 6PH

www.arcadiabooks.co.uk

First published in the United Kingdom 2021
Originally published in French as *Les Exilés du paradis* by PortaParole 2017
Copyright © Brigitte Adès 2021
English translation © Iain Watson and Rosie Capell 2021

ISBN 978-1-911350-79-8

Typeset in Garamond by MacGuru Ltd
Printed and bound by Severn Ltd, Ashville Industrial Estate,
Bristol Road, Gloucester, GL2 5EU, United Kingdom

ARCADIA BOOKS DISTRIBUTORS ARE AS FOLLOWS:

in the UK and elsewhere in Europe:
BookSource
50 Cambuslang Road
Cambuslang
Glasgow G32 8NB

in USA/Canada:
BookMasters
Baker & Taylor
30 Amberwood Parkway
Ashland, OH 44805
USA

in Australia/New Zealand:
NewSouth Books
University of New South Wales
Sydney NSW 2052

To all the Iranians, largely misunderstood,
and to Nader, who first made me discover their world.

EXILES FROM PARADISE

I

Farhad stopped to observe the sky. His eyes followed a few dispersing clouds.

An unpleasant feeling had taken hold of him.

He had felt a stranger in Paris, the city where he had spent most of his life, and he had sought reassurance. The sky was deep blue, just as in Tehran when the wind brought fresh air down from the mountains; just as in New York when in the early mornings he gazed through the peaks of the skyscrapers. This sky was the link that connected all his lives.

He recognised this unease, but let it overcome him for the first time. He stood still, for fear that this newfound aspect of himself might fade away again. It made him feel wholly present.

Before, he had never listened to himself. He had had to silence many voices in order to succeed. Now, at twenty-four, he had come back with a degree from a top American university and had been offered jobs that were difficult to refuse.

Farhad turned to face the passers-by. These four years

of absence allowed him to see his surroundings with fresh eyes. His pale face and his thick black hair gave him a distinctive look. His face tensed slightly. He shivered at the thought of one day being part of this impassive crowd insensitive to the life in the trees. These bystanders came from various countries, yet they formed a homogeneous mass. If by some magic a genie had whisked them away to any other world capital, they would not have been out of place. They themselves would probably not have noticed.

He was reluctant to resume his walk. As people jostled past him, he wobbled before taking up his rapid stride. He felt better instantly, having decided to make space in his life for this other self.

The Champs Elysées stretched out before him. As he left the Rond Point and headed towards Place de la Concorde, he noticed the chestnut trees above him and he felt the urge to reach up and touch a few of the remaining flowers. In America, he wouldn't have hesitated. Here, he knew how to act more constrained and mature. As he passed by the Théâtre Marigny, he considered aloud that it had been four years since he last saw a play. He stopped in front of the Champs-Elysées-Clemenceau metro station and looked at his watch: 2 p.m. He felt a hand on his shoulder.

'Hey!'

Farhad turned around. His gaze was met by a sincere, earnest look. The two men hugged for a few seconds.

'You haven't changed,' said Bardia in his deep voice.

'At our age, it's on the inside that we change the most,' Farhad responded with a smile.

'Come on, they're all waiting!' Bardia said as he led Farhad towards Avenue Franklin Roosevelt.

Sitting around two terraced tables at Le Grand Palais café, their friends were waving them over. They all got up at once and crowded around Farhad.

'When did you get back?'

'Just arrived. I still feel a bit dazed. I didn't sleep on the plane.'

'Exercise is the best way to combat jetlag,' suggested Kamran, a vivacious young Iranian.

'You're right, and I've barely walked from the Etoile to here… It's so great to see you all! What's up?'

'Here, nothing much' Kamran replied. 'But you must have had amazing experiences. Life must be so different over there.'

'Completely different, I was so glad to leave, you have no idea.' As soon as the words slipped out of his mouth, Farhad regretted them, seeing the disappointment on their faces. He tried to explain.

'I missed Paris so much. But just now, for a minute, I got this feeling that I no longer belonged here either.'

'You never fail to surprise me,' said Kamran.

'Here we were, expecting to find an over-confident student, well, an American,' teased Vincent, the only native Frenchman of his high school friends.

'I'm so happy to see you again, even with your sarcasm,' sighed Farhad. 'But I hope you didn't wait for me to order,' he added looking at the packed tables.

'You kidding?' snickered Vincent whose light brown

hair stood out against the others. 'I haven't got much time, I have to be back at the office by half past three.'

'Don't worry, we know you're always in high demand,' joked Farhad as he ordered a rib steak and fries.

It had always been easy to take the mickey out of Vincent.

Their table bubbled with excitement. His friends had broad smiles on their faces, and you could sense their happiness. Farhad was determined to make the most of this reunion.

'How about you guys?' Farhad asked, looking cheerfully over to Cyrus and Teymour.

'We're out of work right now,' admitted Cyrus, looking into his lap.

'How come?' asked Farhad in surprise.

'It's not like we haven't tried everything,' said Teymour defensively. 'We get part-time contracts but nothing permanent. Bosses here are reluctant to take people on because of the risk of severance payments. Plus, our Iranian names don't help.'

Farhad went quiet for a moment. While he had been away, he had idealised France and he had always planned on settling there once he graduated. He was a little disconcerted to hear that even the best students from the Condorcet school, who had got places at prestigious universities, could have such limited career prospects.

'Who cares. After a few tough years, we'll start up our own company. I've got it all planned out,' said Farhad optimistically.

'But you haven't told us why you left the US!' exclaimed Kamran. 'We've all dreamed of going to California. It's like Iran without the mullahs!'

'Even before I went there I knew that I didn't want to stay forever. And my experience didn't change my mind. There is a lot of prejudice in America. You're better off here.'

Everyone nodded.

'You're right. Though France has its difficulties, at least here nobody's on the street from one day to next,' agreed Vincent, looking for approval from the others.

Farhad was about to respond when Bardia interrupted. 'Has anyone heard from Reza? Did no one tell him to come?'

Farhad had already noticed Reza's absence. Even though he could be quite difficult, Reza had always been his closest friend.

'Nobody knows. He moved out of the blue and cut ties with everyone. Even his parents don't have a clue where he is.'

'Maybe he's found someone?' Farhad wondered aloud.

'That's not it,' Kamran said. 'I've seen him going into the mosque a few times. I think he's got a job there…'

Farhad started. The news hit him like a ton of bricks.

There was a pause.

'So you still live right next to the great mosque?' he asked Kamran, trying to keep his composure.

'Reza? At the mosque? What's got into him?' cried Cyrus.

'He's not the first this has happened to, as you know,' Teymour said. 'If Reza wants to practise his religion, we shouldn't make a big deal out of it. It doesn't necessarily mean he'll turn out to be a fundamentalist.'

Kamran shared his thoughts. 'Reza must have had his lot of disappointments, just like the rest of us. At school they told us that if we worked hard, we'd be sure of a bright future. We all played the game. We were brought up on Western culture, we know their philosophers, their writers, as well as they do. But we're still thought of as foreigners, when all we want is to find our place here.'

'Sure we do, like most people. But you know well it's the vocal minority who gets the spotlight and then we're all painted in a bad light,' Cyrus observed.

'The worst mistake you can make is to let them speak for all of you,' cried Vincent. 'If none of you is brave enough to stand up to them…'

The conversation continued in this vein. Over the past four years, they had become adults.

As he left, Farhad was deep in thought. Economic segregation was clearly unacceptable, but joining the radicals wasn't going to help their public image.

He decided he would arrange as soon as possible a catch-up with Reza, who had failed to answer friendship's call.

II

Farhad's first night was restless. His bed felt too narrow. He had got used to American proportions. The ambience of his room, which he had so often dreamed of, wasn't as he recalled it. In a moment of insomnia, he thought of renewing his Iranian passport. The Institute of Global Affairs had asked him to write a report about Iran. Why not take them up on it? His expenses would be covered, and he hadn't been back since he was a child. Now was the time.

With this thought, he eventually fell asleep late into the night, and awoke to the sound of the front door gently being closed. Drawn by the smell of coffee and toast his mother had made, he stumbled out to the kitchen. He took his time: the first meal of the day would be crucial to help him recover from jetlag. He woke up properly once he was in the shower. Then he came out and walked naked down the corridor, his athletic body almost too wide for the narrow walls. He pulled a pair of jeans and an old blazer from his cupboard, for a look that would maintain his style without raising the eyebrows of the bearded embassy staff.

He went out into the street. The locals gave him slightly

surprised looks, as if they were wondering which woman in the building this dark, handsome man had spent the night with.

As he was about to push open the gate of the embassy railings, a familiar voice called out to him.

'Farhad Safandar, what brings you here?'

Farhad turned to face Mansour Dalavandi. This friend of his father's had always shown an interest in his development. He was stunned to see him outside of the walls which he had refused to enter since the revolution.

'What a surprise! What have you come to the mullahs for? Are you back for good?'

'Yes, I have a few job offers, but I want to take a bit of time out.'

This man who hated pretences looked him straight in the eyes and reiterated, 'I hope you're not thinking of going back to Iran?'

'I might take a short trip there to do some research, which is why I need my Iranian passport.'

'Don't rush into anything! And if you do go, don't stay too long or you might end up meeting a beautiful girl who'll persuade you to stay.'

'I'll think of you if ever I'm tempted to peek under a chador.'

Remembering that he was also Reza's uncle, Farhad asked him for news of his family.

'My aunt has just passed away. Come along to her memorial next Wednesday,' he said. 'We would love to see you there.'

Farhad promised he'd be there and excused himself.

An hour later he left the embassy. His passport would arrive in a matter of days.

The following week, Farhad pondered the roles of fate and destiny as he climbed the few steps up to Mr Dalavandi's apartment. Their chance encounter had given him a good excuse to see Reza, whom he still hadn't heard from. What was he up to?

As soon as he rang the bell, the door opened and a man in a black suit asked him in. There was a low hum of conversation in the background. A large bouquet of white flowers was wilting in the heat on a Venetian console table. He caught sight of an elderly lady from behind as she was about to go into the living room. Farhad placed his hand on her arm. He had recognised her as his great-aunt Nasrine, a dear friend of the deceased. Their two families had owned neighbouring holiday homes on the Caspian Sea, where they used to spend their summers.

'What are you doing here, my dear?' she asked as they embraced. 'I thought you were still in America!'

Farhad's heart melted as he smelled the familiar perfume that she had been wearing since he was a child.

'I've finished university, Auntie.'

Farhad hadn't seen his aunt since he had left for the US. He felt how frail she had become and promised to visit her in the coming days.

They sat down next to each other in the living room,

with some Darjeeling tea and delicate halva cakes that had been made for the wake.

Visitors came in and took a seat on the chairs that had been set out along the walls. No one said a word. They all reflected in silence, simply nodding in acknowledgement as new arrivals came in. As it was customary not to stay long, Farhad was the first to stand up and take his leave. He had reached the hallway when two strong arms hugged him from behind.

'Farhad, home at last!'

Ordinarily a little reserved and restrained, today Reza's face was lit up with a big smile. He led Farhad over to the corner of the room and told him how much he had hated this last year in Paris. His work hadn't lived up to expectations and his contract hadn't been renewed. He became more animated as he described how one day, he had felt the need to recharge his batteries, so had gone to the Paris mosque.

'I spoke to the others in the prayer room; intense people who are staunch in their beliefs. Some of them are scholars. All of them are open to learning. I go regularly now. My parents disapprove; they've cut me out.'

'You can understand why,' said Farhad. 'Our families have always been wary of religious groups, although they respect tradition.'

Reza explained that he would soon be leaving for a new job in London, as treasurer of a charitable foundation financed by wealthy Saudi Arabian families.

'These people's generosity is astonishing,' he exclaimed.

'They already donate two fifths of their income to the poor, as the Quran instructs.'

'Where does this money go?' asked Farhad.

'Often to refugee camps. I have done some research and they are everywhere; in Yemen, Lebanon, Egypt, Syria… It just goes to show how open these people are.'

'Aside from that, are you still with your French girlfriend?'

'No, you know, I've lost interest in women. Well, sort of…' said Reza. 'In any case, I don't ever see myself with a Western spouse.'

Farhad couldn't hide his surprise. All this from Reza, who had only ever been seen with European girls…

Reza continued jokingly, 'And English girls aren't going to persuade me otherwise!'

They laughed heartily together as if they had never been apart. Farhad promised to visit Reza in London soon.

The following afternoon, Farhad went to see his great-aunt.

'I was expecting you,' said Nasrine, as he came in.

The coffee table was full of his favourite desserts. His aunt wasn't the slightest bit annoyed that he had been gone so long. They sat side by side on the sofa. Beneath his adult features, as she looked at him, she could see the face of the child she knew so well: a mixture of innocence and loyalty, a face that didn't hide anything, where his emotions were always on display. His heart had not been tarnished by his time in America. Nasrine had never forgiven the Americans for abandoning Iran in 1979.

'You're looking a little off, my boy.' She could read him like a book.

Farhad nodded and looked at her with clear blue eyes.

When he was small, he used to spend long periods at his aunt's when his parents were off on their travels. He loved staying at her house near Isfahan, where he felt free in the grand garden, with its shaded roses bushes and ponds where symmetrical rivulets fed the trickling fountains. He could spend hours there playing the same game; dropping a petal on each parallel current to see which would get there first. He enjoyed following them from above as they were transported silently, passing slabs of marble and landing in the pond at the end. Sometimes the breeze would induce a spiral along the way, giving or taking away the advantage of one petal over the other. Without those little dapples of colour, the water would have seemed completely still.

As he contemplated his fond childhood memories, one in particular came back to him. One afternoon, when he was six years old, he had gone to find his aunt to ask permission not to go back to school. Why did he have to be torn away from his games? Why did he have to waste so much time sitting in class, when he could be running around the garden, observing the insects and the plants? And his great-aunt could teach him so much! She had given him an amused look and had taken his pain seriously. She set out her conditions: she would let him stay home that afternoon if he read two chapters of the book of kings, the *Shahnahmeh*, aloud with her. Together they would then choose two passages in verse to memorise.

When he agreed to this, the boy had not realised how much she was demanding in exchange for an afternoon off school. Farhad had always remembered reading about the adventures of Rostam, the splendid warrior, who was the epitome of accomplishment. This epic hero had left his mark on Farhad's imagination. As he recalled this scene, he felt more relaxed than he had been for a long time.

Farhad had neglected his Iranian origins during his time at university. And his mother had brought only one Saadi book from Iran, determined as she was to integrate into France, their host country.

As he smelled the scent of the rose petals and tucked into cardamom cakes, Farhad asked about their family. He wanted to know about his ancestors' lives. But he didn't want to hear about the tragic story of his grandfather, Commander-in-Chief of the Shah's Air Force, who had been considered one of the few officers capable of overturning the new regime. This man, one of the first Iranians to graduate with honours from West Point Military Academy, had been executed in the early days of the revolution. Apart from him, Farhad knew nothing about his family.

His aunt needed no encouragement.

The Safandar family boasted many colourful individuals: a philosopher who turned his back on his responsibilities and lived out his life as a hermit; several politicians who had sat in Parliament and defended the first constitutional

revolution to limit the power of the Qadjar kings; others
who had served with the Shah in wars in India; Darius
and his brothers who had made a name for themselves
while helping to unify the country during the time of the
Safavids, such as in the battle against the Ottomans. His
great uncle Jamshid, by contrast, was a collector of miniatures and had squandered his family's wealth with his
extravagant living.

'Did you know that our family is one of the oldest in
Persia? Our ancestor, Nader the Elder, was a great servant
of our country.'

Farhad stopped chewing his pistachio nougat for a
second.

'Mum has never said anything about that. She wants to
break all ties with our Iranian past.'

'I don't think your mother knows what I am about to
tell you,' she said. 'It's a secret which is meant to skip a
generation each time it's passed down. Have you heard of
the Sect of the Assassins?'

'I remember hearing something about it. They threatened the stability of Persia for some time.'

'Yes. It was during the reign of the Sunnite Seljuks,
the first great Eastern dynasty of Turkey. Nader the
Elder was one of the most fervent opponents of Hassan
Sabbah, the founder of the sect. They knew each other
when they were younger. They'd formed a small group
with Omar Khayyam and a certain Nizam, who was a
few years older and was to become the most influential man in the kingdom. The boys had taken an oath

to always help each other out. They all loved learning, and Hassan was by far the most erudite. When they used to meet at Nishapur, where they were born, they would discuss literature, history and politics. His friends all had a special place in Nader's heart. Later they found themselves in Isfahan when it was pronounced capital of the Persian Empire. By then, they had extraordinary careers. Omar Khayyam was already a great poet and had made a name for himself as a mathematician and astronomer. Nizam was vizier to Malik Shah of the Seljuks dynasty, while Hassan, great voyager and fervent Ismailian, had been trained in Nizarism in Egypt before coming back to Isfahan. In his memoirs, Nader the Elder writes that he met Hassan when he had just been named court treasurer on the recommendation of their friend Nizam. Despite this, after just a few months, Hassan had plotted against Nizam while seeking the favour of Malik Shah. He suggested to the king that he could complete an audited budget of the kingdom within forty days, when he knew well Nizam would take a year to submit it. Nizam foiled this plot and had Hassan dismissed.'

Nasrine paused.

'Are you following me so far, my dear?'

'Perfectly, Auntie, please go on.'

Satisfied, his aunt continued. She explained how after this humiliation, Hassan bore a deep-rooted grudge against the Seljuk court, and would not rest until he had destroyed the dynasty. To that end, he formed a secret society, surrounding himself with devotees and organising training camps

in his fortress. He created fanatics whom he wouldn't hesitate to kill in order to assert his authority. One day, he told
his most faithful follower to jump from the high Alamut
wall. Knowing that he was facing certain death, the soldier
looked up towards Hassan. A wave of sadness passed across
his eyes, but he obeyed without a word. From that day on,
Nader became his greatest enemy. These crimes triggered a
merciless war between them. Hassan Sabbah, the self-pro-
claimed Grand Master of the sect, would commit many
murderous deeds. He would never fail, because his followers did not fear death. If they survived their mission, the
fanatics let themselves be captured, certain of their place in
heaven. Feared across the Empire, they became known as
the 'Sect of Assassins'. Hassan Sabbah would attack many
Persian political leaders. He had his old friend Nizam
killed, and then the Shah himself. Followers continued to
be recruited throughout the Middle East.

'The sect became so powerful,' continued Nasrine, 'that
four impenetrable fortresses were constructed in the space
of a few years.'

'And our ancestor managed to defeat that bloodthirsty
brute!' exclaimed Farhad.

'Not exactly, but he was the first to take a stand against
him. It took four generations and fierce battles for them
to finally be overcome.'

Eventually, in 1256, a descendant of Nader the Elder
contributed to the fall of Alamut fortress, which had a
vast library.

When the last bastion was taken by force, its immediate

destruction was ordered. The famous historian Ata Malik Djovayni, whose job it was to chronicle these battles, writes that he begged the victor, Mughal Khan Hulagu, to spare the library. The monarch agreed to save as many books as could be carried on the back of a donkey, in recognition of his historian's loyal service.

That was how the destruction of this temple of knowledge was delayed. Farhad imagined the dilemma faced by the historian as he rushed down the shelves, forced to choose between masterpieces, and horrified at the thought of sacrificing so many sources of learning which would be lost forever.

Farhad didn't tire of listening to his aunt, rather he took full advantage of it. With each word she spoke, he was immersed in his country's history. He suddenly realised that he came from Persia, his spiritual home, a place of learning and values. His links to this land became clear to him. Captivated by this account of the birth of warrior mysticism, he had an idea of how he could renew his bond with this land.

'And this whole story is told by our ancestor in his memoirs?' he asked, astounded.

'Yes, and many other things besides,' answered his aunt.

'But where are the memoirs?'

'In Isfahan, hidden in a crypt beneath our house. I got to read them thanks to my great uncle Darius, who taught me just as I am teaching you.'

Once he had heard that story, it became essential to Farhad that he read the memoirs. He saw his aunt in a new light. She had maintained her imposing demeanour and her darting eyes were always ready to surprise. He complimented her on having kept her wisdom in exile.

'How did you bear such a radical change of lifestyle?'

She looked straight at him with an authoritative expression.

'I didn't change my life. None of this is important,' she said, gracefully gesturing to her relatively modest home. 'It is our duty to be thankful for what we have, when so many are suffering and deprived of their rights in our country. "Freedom is not doing what you want, but wanting to do what is right," a philosopher once said. I forget who it was – a disciple of Kant, perhaps.'

While she was talking, she had gone to find a little hand-drawn map which she passed to him. Farhad looked at it closely, asking for details about the location of the crypt and how to access it. Then he got up to leave. She insisted on showing him out. He kissed her on both cheeks and left with a heavy heart. He chastised himself for having stayed so long, no doubt tiring her with his visit.

Once he was in the street, Farhad headed towards the Commission for European Affairs. It now seemed indispensable to take a few months out. He suddenly felt a strong urge to go to Iran. His mother would understand. He had spent all these years immersed in his work with hordes of able students whose destiny was all mapped out, built on entrance exams and scholarships. 'He is going through a belated teenage identity crisis,' his mother would say. What did that matter.

He carried on walking at a sustained but comfortable pace.

He left behind the Esplanade du Trocadéro, and reached the Place de l'Alma in no time, following the twists and turns of the Seine to the Alexandre III bridge. Here he crossed over to the left bank and headed to Les Invalides, then, less than five minutes later, he was on the Rue de l'Université.

When he arrived, a secretary asked him to wait in the foyer. The door was ajar and Farhad could see his mother alone in this large panelled room. She was on the phone behind her Louis XV-style desk. When she saw him, she gave a delighted smile and gestured for him to wait. She looked down and continued her conversation.

In her late fifties, she was a beautiful woman. Her hair fell halfway down her shoulders. She had a pale, delicate complexion, and deep black eyes with a touch of make-up. As soon as she hung up, Farhad rushed over to her.

'Mum, I've just been to Auntie Nasrine's,' he said.

'How is she?' she asked as she lifted her reading glasses to kiss him.

'A little tired, but sharp as always.'

'She's incredible for her age,' his mother said, her eyes bursting with pride.

'Did you know our ancestors fought against the Sect of the Assassins?'

'No, I didn't, but if you want to talk about family, let's do it another time…'

In her opinion, her son should have been focusing on other priorities and thinking about his future.

'The Agha Khan is still the spiritual representative of the Ismailia sect, the direct descendants of the Assassins. He might be able to give you some insight. Let me know if you want to meet him.'

Since her son had returned to Paris, she had made it her mission to introduce him to influential people.

'No, I'd rather go back to Isfahan, to explore our past.'

'You can't be serious! With a name like ours, your passport will be confiscated. You won't be allowed to leave. I know people who were detained for weeks.'

Farhad didn't answer. Maryam looked her son straight in the eyes. He seemed defiant. She had never seen this expression on his face, and she had trouble controlling herself. This was the first time that he had stood up to her. The fear of seeing her son return to Iran, of seeing him question the bonds to the West that she had worked so hard to instil, was too much to bear. She started to lose her temper.

'I'm worried about you. When companies see you're going back to Iran, they won't take you on.'

Farhad stayed quiet, fixing her with an intense gaze. He suddenly saw her as fragile and felt a strong wave of love for his mother. He wished he could reason her out of the absurd convictions on which her life in France was founded. She had chosen to ignore her origins in order to better immerse herself in the culture of this new country. That was her choice. It was up to him to prove that it was possible to build a bridge between these two worlds without careering off course. At that moment, he sensed that she would not approve of his new life, but he was ready. At twenty-four years old, he was no longer under her thumb.

'I have been taken on by Yale Institute's Department of International Affairs,' he continued, in order to calm her down. 'They need experts on Iran.'

He added that he would have permission to publish extracts of his research on the website of the Council on Foreign Relations, or in the *New Yorker*, with whom they had publications agreements. Who knows? Maybe there'd even be a book.

Knowing that his director of studies had offered to fund a trip to write a report on Iran, and that it would be read by influential people, she was slightly reassured, and resigned herself to his leaving.

III

On the flight to Tehran, Farhad could finally relax. Only a few days had elapsed between his decision to take the trip and his departure. The plane shuddered as they took off. He remembered the ban on the sale of aircraft and spare parts that had long been in place in Iran. Yet he knew that, although they had many hours of air travel behind them, the planes of Iran Air were well-maintained. He looked around. Some of the women, including the air hostesses, were wearing the Islamic hijab, the chador. Most had ignored these directives, like the cheery and slightly sturdy lady sitting next to him with a young boy. Farhad had offered her the window seat, with typically Persian politeness. She had smiled while pointing out how energetic the little boy was, running down the aisle as he almost knocked into a sour-looking man walking past.

'He's a civil guard,' the lady explained as she leaned towards him. 'They have two or three on every flight. You can spot them a mile off.'

Too busy suppressing the worries that were threatening to drown him, Farhad did not answer. He focused all his energy on reading Rumi, the Persian mystic poet. He hadn't opened this book in nine years. When he was given it as a present, he'd merely flicked through a few pages before putting it away. At the age of fifteen, he hadn't quite grasped the importance of this thinker. Now, he was looking for a poem that would help allay his fears. On page forty, a title caught his eye: 'Unfold your own myth.'

He read:

Unfold your own myth simply, without explanation,
So that all can understand the passage,
'We have opened you.'
Start walking towards Shams, your legs will get heavy
And tired. Then will come a moment
Of feeling the wings you have grown
Lifting.

He closed the book and looked out of the cabin window. Neither Persian mystics, nor his mother, would help him find his way. A break in the clouds gave him a glimpse of the Aegean Sea. Perhaps he would soon spot Rhodes, then the Turkish coast. It fascinated him to think that these places were so close. He went over the great historical moments that had shaped these countries: The Knights of Rhodes; the Temple of Apollo at Delphi, which bore the inscription 'Know thyself' and beneath, 'Nothing to excess' to encourage moderation; the Trojan Wars; the *Iliad*. They all blurred into a dream as he fell asleep, his mother's disapproving but well-meaning voice echoing in his mind.

After a few hours he was woken up by the woman next to him. She apologised for knocking him as she rummaged through a bag on her lap. Eventually she pulled out a long, crumpled item of clothing and a headscarf. He looked around the plane. Other women were busy putting on rain-coats or jackets to hide their bodies. They were all covering up. They wrapped scarves over their heads. Some dressed in black started to look like birds of ill omen. Farhad shivered. His eyes fixed on the window, he refused to give in to the worries mounting inside him. Only a few minutes to go before landing. The lights of Tehran were shining through the night sky. He could make out the Alborz mountain range which, standing at six thousand metres tall, created a natural barrier between the Caspian Sea and the vast, slightly sloped plains of central Iran. The city had spread out. Lights were scattered across the surrounding hills. 'At least the landscape hasn't changed,' he said to himself with a fondness that reduced his anxiety at returning to his hometown after all these years of Islamic rule.

As soon as he stepped out onto the footbridge, Farhad felt better. Breathing in the fresh, cool night air reassured him, and took him back to the summer evenings of his childhood. He hurried down the steps, determined not to let the changes in his country get to him.

'Salam aleykoum Agha.'

As Farhad said these first words, the officer looked up in surprise. His pronunciation clearly showed that he had been away for some time. The man opened his passport and returned it to him without a word.

His fear of getting his passport confiscated was allayed. He wouldn't have been the first returning exile to be grilled. The stories people told in France about their entanglements with the secret police were terrible. Some had only got their passports back on the day of their departure.

Farhad picked up his suitcase and passed through a security barrier. Someone gestured for him to stop. He had forgotten to fill out a form. The amicable customs officer offered to do it for him. When Farhad mentioned that he had not been back in eighteen years, the officer waved him through with a friendly 'welcome back'.

Farhad was touched. But he frowned as he saw the long line of people on the other side of the frosted-glass sliding door. As he was head and shoulders above most of the passengers, he could see what was causing this delay. With arms full of bouquets of flowers, families were blocking the exit with their reunions. It was a local custom to come in great numbers to meet loved ones at the airport. The passengers, some still looking sleepy, had to endure this as soon as they passed through the gate. At this time of night, the din was quite surprising.

Farhad waited patiently. He needed to adapt to this new rhythm and keep his cool. He managed to squeeze his way past and as soon as he was outside, he was relieved to jump into a taxi. He gave the address of his hotel to the driver.

Tehran was unrecognisable. Haphazard constructions made the city look confused. Overpasses were everywhere and even at this time of night the traffic was heavy. He knew that the local population had increased from three to fourteen million in less than twenty years. They passed through very lively neighbourhoods: the population came to life at night to avoid the daytime summer heat.

The next morning, as soon as he stepped outside, Farhad was pleased to feel Tehran's perfect temperature. He hadn't planned on staying in the town for long, but he felt the urge to revisit the streets he had walked down as a child.

He had reserved a taxi to take him to Isfahan. Before they got onto the motorway, he asked the driver to take a detour into the centre of town. The streets were just as cheerful as the night before. He was struck by how many young people there were. Hundreds of dark-headed pedestrians walked along the pavements. It was still the summer holidays and everyone was outside. There was laughter and joking, and the young women were dressed in bright colours. With the new post-revolutionary street names, Farhad didn't recognise any of them and it was impossible for him to get his bearings. Suddenly the taxi turned onto the former Pahlavi Avenue, now renamed 'Valiasr', the Master of Time, after the twelfth Shiite imam. He couldn't resist asking the driver to stop.

For the first time in weeks, he felt comfortable. He looked up and took in the immense oriental plane trees. They would live through more regime changes. He set off into the crowd of people to get a closer look. The flowing cotton skirts and shirts went from blues to greens to scarlet reds, reminiscent of eternal Persian folklore. He felt that this was a dedicated people, with a strong sense of heritage that had remained untouched by the West. Suddenly he had a craving for melon juice. He remembered a place that used to sell it near the bazaar.

This peaceful moment was broken by raised voices: a member of the morality police was reprimanding a young woman whom he thought hadn't covered up enough. He demanded to see her papers. She answered coldly, with a reproachful look. He threatened to take her to the station. Everyone's face tensed. The cheeriness had disappeared. The officer got her to adjust her headscarf, and then turned on his heel without saying a word. Farhad watched the officer as he spoke to some men further away. 'Am I paranoid or are they plain-clothed police?' he wondered. He shivered at the thought of the danger young women faced with their personal interpretations of the chador. Some of them were wearing sandals, with painted nails, and their headscarf halfway down their heads. 'They've got courage,' he thought. This was the paradox of the current regime.

He carried on walking through the crowds. Most of them seemed to embody a *joie de vivre*, despite their derisory wages. It was said that some family breadwinners had to work several jobs to make ends meet. He stopped in front of a bakery window where pastries and cakes were on display. He ordered a rose ice cream, which he was very fond of. He attempted to catch the eyes of the people at the tables to start a conversation, but he was worried about how they would react. He didn't want them to take him for a foreigner. The young man behind him also ordered a rose ice cream. While they were waiting to be served, their eyes met and they smiled, both waiting to taste the wonderfully gentle yet sour flavour, so indicative of the contrasts of their country.

He walked back to the taxi, content with his ice cream. He gestured to the driver and got in, apologising for making him wait. On the journey, for the first time ever he appreciated the Persian music playing on the radio. As he settled into the seat, the driver asked, 'Where do you come from?'

'How do you know I don't live here?'

'From your accent, sir. If I may, your vocabulary and even your pronunciation are slightly different. You speak like we used to under the old regime.'

'I used to live in Shemiran, in the Zaferanieh neighbourhood.'

'That area has been transformed. Many of the houses were demolished to make way for apartment blocks. Shall we go up there?'

Farhad declined. A memory came back to him as he said the name of his old neighbourhood. He recalled the Friday evenings at his grandmother's where the extended family would get together, as part of a tradition. She had told him that when he was a child, his father had loved picking at the food that was laid out for the buffet, while the adults privately discussed and settled affairs of state. It greatly saddened his grandmother that these family get-togethers had become a rarity after the tragic revolution.

In that neighbourhood, Farhad had seen the deserted houses that his mother had pointed out to him as she listed all the family friends who were now in exile.

They left the town and headed south, moving away from the Alborz mountains. Those mountains, which had such a presence in the town, had always been mysterious to Farhad. He had heard countless peculiar stories of how these mountainous kingdoms had been a sanctuary for exiled Ismailians and Shiite dissidents over the centuries.

Soon they reached the desert on the way to Isfahan. Farhad leaned back, resting his head on the imitation leather headrest. He woke up, a little drowsy, once they had passed Qom, the religious town. They were making headway through the countryside.

Farhad was fascinated by the scenery. The Iraq war seemed to have left this region untouched. The women that he could see out herding were wearing traditional dresses, and even from a distance there were so beautiful! As he caught just a glimpse of their colourful clothes, Farhad enjoyed the thought that they were perhaps not wearing veils. He remembered learning in school about how when Reza Shah took power in 1925, he had discouraged the wearing of the chador, and how his son Mohammed Reza, the last Shah, had even redistributed land in 1963 to the farmers, disadvantaging large landowners including his own family. It was the 'white' revolution.

The Shah had, however, given financial compensation for this expropriation while allowing landowners to retain their houses and a hectare of land. The Safandars, who were always respected and well-liked, were still considered lords, even now, fifty years on.

He had been told that each year, in the middle of autumn, his grandmother drove from village to village, accompanied by her entourage. In the evenings, once her huge tent was erected on a flattened floor covered with thick carpets, she greeted the local dignitaries who had come to share their concerns about the upkeep of the village. In her vast circular pavilion, surrounded by her refined furniture and vases fragrant with rare perfumes, she discussed burst pipes, shattered roofs and offered to finance the most urgent repairs. If she ran into a wedding, his grandmother distributed gold coins and provided a trousseau of fine linen for the bride. Accompanied by her son, Farhad's father, who loved these outings, she drove an immense pink Cadillac herself. He enjoyed recalling that she had been the first woman to drive in Iran.

Farhad then remembered her, still radiant, in the narrow Paris apartment. Overcoming her grief, she had managed to find a renewed sense of harmony in life. New friends, exiled Iranians and Europeans, were always happy to meet at her place.

Farhad jumped up in his seat: they were arriving in one of his grandmother's former villages. Instinctively, he closed his eyes to avoid any disappointment. But the aroma of the flowering jasmine and honeysuckle wafting through the open car window enticed him to open them: the same flowers covered the walls of patrician houses. It was market day and the cars were driven at the pace of pedestrians in the narrow lanes, built that way to encourage contact between people. In these houses, two internal courtyards protected families so that neither raised voices nor family squabbles would be heard outside.

Once they passed the village square with its aromas of spicy dishes, he was anxious to get to the family house and garden. Less than five kilometres separated him from the most cherished place of his entire life. What would it be like today?

He had no time to dwell on his emotions. Catching sight of the tall cypress trees which lined the driveway, he was filled with joy. It was still light. He recognised the simple architecture of that vast building, the Safandar's bastion, and its wings, preceded by a long rectangular pool. He wanted to ask the chauffeur to let him walk the last few hundred metres but the car was already passing through the open gate. There was a silhouette in front of the main entrance.

A man of around sixty was waiting for him. It was Hachem, the gardener, who now owned the house. Hachem studied Farhad intently, trying to find a trace of a family resemblance in his gait, his youthful face, and his clear eyes under thick eyebrows. But he was interrupted by Farhad who warmly embraced him. Wasn't it Hachem who had taught him botany and how to play football? Hadn't there been countless afternoons when he'd helped Farhad hide to avoid studying?

Very respectfully, Hachem pulled away and kissed the

hand of his former master's son before showing him into the house. A plethora of memories came back to Farhad at the sight of the familiar cracks in the entrance hall, which would always transform into parchment maps in his childhood imagination.

He strode confidently through the main gallery, where the smell of saffron rice scented the air. But he started back when he saw a woman in a chador working at the back of the large kitchen. She was the gardener's new wife, and she had been expecting them. She had prepared a lavish traditional meal. In Iran, hospitality is sacrosanct.

Hachem took his guest into the garden before dinner, as daylight was quickly fading. He had a surprise for him. In his shed, the gardener had kept some of the family's treasured possessions: tennis racquets, bridles and polo mallets, the croquet set, his first bicycle and most importantly, Rahsht, his little rocking horse. 'The hardest thing was keeping my children away from them!' he laughed. He seemed relieved to finally be able to show his allegiance to a member of the household whose life he had so enjoyed sharing.

Farhad was touched by the way this simple-hearted man had cared for these relics, which had lost their lustre with the passing of time, in what resembled a personal museum of a bygone era. It seemed to him that his family had been put on a pedestal by a man who had refused to adapt to the new political landscape. Farhad understood the power of the feudal spirit and empathised with the pain Hachem must have had to bear over the previous twenty years. While Farhad had lived in Europe and his family had set about their new life abroad, their gardener had stayed behind, a guardian of the past, trapped in his memories.

There was a silent pause as Farhad marvelled over his old toys, then, putting the lid back on his emotions, he asked after Hachem's second wife. Since he was a widower, in order to avoid being harassed and evicted after the family had gone, Hachem had been strongly advised to take a new wife of impeccable political and religious convictions. He had chosen Zahra, the daughter of a Revolutionary Guard, who had given him two children.

Dinner in the enormous kitchen went as well as possible under the slightly inquisitorial gaze of the gardener's wife. Yet, as soon as anecdotes from the past began to surface, and the bond between the two men became too apparent, her expression turned from astonishment to contempt. When an overexcited Hachem got onto the real problems in the country and began loudly expressing his nostalgia for the old monarchy, Farhad changed the subject.

'It's a good thing I am only staying one night,' he said to himself as he got up from the table. 'Otherwise, my host might get into trouble.'

Hachem had tried to insist that his guest sleep on the first floor, but instead Farhad had chosen one of the rooms on the ground floor filled with memories of happy times with his cousins. Two of the French windows opened out onto the garden. He went out. The tiered fountains were still there in front of him. They had just been turned on. The pleasant tinkling of the water immediately welcomed him as he stepped outside.

Back in his room, Farhad decided he would not sleep that night.

He lay with his eyes closed, listening to the soothing chorus of toads and other familiar nocturnal sounds. For two hours, he relived the key moments of his life: his childhood in this enchanting house; the shock of being forced into exile; his studies in France and America. And the moment when he suddenly felt an unexplained yearning to return; an urge that could prove crucial to his passage into adulthood. As memories came flooding back, a sharp pain took hold of him for a second. Farhad observed a link between these pangs and his efforts to adapt to his new life.

This was all bound up with a feeling of nostalgia for a lost paradise, an attachment to his childhood, to his life in Iran. All the buried experiences that had been integral to his development came back to him in lifelike intensity. His raids of the hen houses when he pinched eggs, and the chicks who huddled together as he came towards them. His love for Palang, the German Shepherd who never tired of following him on his walks and waited patiently as he stopped in front of many bushes, examining every leaf for potential rare insects. Many times he had played the scene of their departure over in his head. He had sugar-coated it in order to suppress it even deeper. This time it appeared in all its harsh, crude reality. Yet another family forced into permanent exile, just like many others through the course of that century. The bloodiest century in history. That cruel truth had always convinced him to muzzle his own grief. After all, had they not been privileged to have had advance warning of their departure? His mother had been able to start a new career and a new life for herself.

Yet today, by finally admitting to this suffering, he was unearthing the psychological fragility that had followed his exile, and so this mental construction was beginning to crumble.

He shook these thoughts off. The house was completely still. He opened the French window and went back out into the night. The sandy soil was lit up by an almost full moon, soon to reach its zenith, which cast no shadows and gave the ground a silvery sheen.

The toads had stopped croaking. In their place, an owl was hooting in the tranquillity of the night. Farhad lifted the barn door latch and was greeted by the acrid odour of damp earth. He started at the creaking of his footsteps on the uneven, dusty floor.

The crypt had to be under the barn. His aunt Nasrine had given him plenty of pointers to help him find the entrance. Every ounce of Farhad's fear was suppressed by a surge of pride as he realised he was one of only a single family member each generation to be party to the secret.

If his calculations were correct, the full moon shining through the skylight would soon light up a precise spot and reveal the entrance. He headed over to the moonlit wall and recognised a faint symbol to the right of the tack hooks. He pressed down on the symbol and the ground shifted to uncover a trap door. Farhad went down the moonlit travertine-marble steps that appeared to be leading to a hidden chamber. The path down there was clear. His small torch brought an oval crypt to life, with its vaulted mosaic ceiling. Everything was perfectly preserved, and the air was clean thanks to good ventilation. Persians, he remembered, had been experts in underground construction since ancient times, and had invented a very sophisticated system of water canals to link houses and even cities together. As he picked out the symbols of his family's crest on the vaulted ceiling, Farhad was stirred for a second. He reflected on the strict education, passed from generation to generation, which had given his family both work ethic and reserve, making them capable of taking on state affairs. Now it was for him to carry the torch. He had to immerse himself in the memoirs and soak them up; there was no time to waste. There was nowhere to sit, so participants must have stayed on their feet through hurried meetings and hushed instructions. The secret assemblies could not be allowed to go beyond those walls.

A thick, dust-covered manuscript awaited him as it had his ancestors before him. The opening pages, with their large, even and elegant Arabic lettering, confirmed these were indeed the memoirs of Nader the Elder. Farhad hoped he would be able to understand it.

His Persian slowly came back to him. In early childhood, he had learned to read and write it. He took the time to decipher the passages already bookmarked by strips of leather, which had stuck together and left a brownish blemish on the page.

Farhad happened upon what he thought was an account of a battle. A second leather strip seemed to mark a political analysis of general interest. Disregarding the leather bookmarks, he decided to choose one passage at random. A few underlined words caught his eye. He could read the highlighted words without difficulty: 'Hassan y Sabbah'. In that passage, Nader the Elder described his three friends, who had been brought together by their passion for philosophy.

An excellent orator, Hassan had read many Greek philosophers as well as Indian and Persian wise men. He was particularly influenced by the writings of the great Avicenna, whose father had been an Ismaili, just like his.

Nader talked about how when he was seventeen, he used to meet up and debate with his friends in Nishapour in the evenings. Hassan, who thought of himself as a Theosophist, had very set ideas about life's mysteries. He was, as yet, far from being the spiritual master of the sect he would later create. That said, he already claimed he had a magnetic power that his friends attributed to a stone which he always carried with him. His father had told him one day about a forty-foot meteorite that had landed on a nearby patch of land a century before. The young boy had taken one of the fragments, ignoring strict instructions not to touch the stone or its scattered debris. This most precious of treasures fascinated him with its shape and density, and fuelled his imagination with thoughts of far-off lands. Nader went on to describe how one evening in May 1102, while the four friends were observing the skies, Hassan had pointed out a comet. Its blazing trajectory, lighting up the sky as it went, was taken by them to be a sign.

Hassan, who thought of himself as an alchemist, had come back a week later with the stone. It had been cut into three parts, and on each one he had engraved a few words. In order to seal their friendship and swear their lifelong commitment to each other, he offered a piece to each of his friends. No one even knew how he had managed to engrave it, let alone cut it.

What Farhad read confirmed what his aunt Nasrine had told him. He skimmed over what he already knew about the extraordinary fortunes of these four friends, but he did notice that his ancestor had been the only one among them to lead his life according to the precepts they had devised together in their youth.

Farhad discovered he was standing in the very same crypt where, some thousand years previously, Nader had called secret meetings to counteract his friend's growing influence, petrified and shocked as he was by the sect's methods and the never-ending assassinations. And even though it had proved impossible to stop him, he succeeded in warning many young men of the harmful influence of the order, and in teaching them not to doubt themselves, but to develop critical thinking founded on their own knowledge and reason. This had proved fairly easy, since

Hassan relied on fallible arguments, using religion like superstition to confuse and manipulate the naive. Indeed, his followers were banned from the immense library he had compiled in his Alamut fortress, in order to keep the truth from them. It was there that he spent all his time, only rarely appearing to his disciples; which reinforced the air of mystery he was constructing for himself.

Farhad lingered over a few sentences at the bottom of the page, signed by Nader's great-grandson who had contributed to the fall of Alamut in 1256. The note revealed that after Hassan had had Nizam, the vizier, stabbed to death, he gave orders to have Nizam's stone stolen from his corpse, and he guarded it in his apartments, where it remained for over two hundred years.

During the great fire, permission was also given to the historian Djovayni to take the apparently insignificant stone. No one but him knew that it held part of the precept that Hassan had drawn up during his youth, and which was integral to his philosophy. It held a particular importance given that all Hassan's written works were lost in the blaze.

As for his ancestor's piece of the stone, the notes confirmed that it had not left the crypt and, according to Nader the Elder's wishes, had been hidden away in a secret recess. All Farhad had to do was to find it. The rest of the text revealed a link between the family crest and a shining point on the star-covered ceiling.

Farhad looked up, on the hunt for further clues. His torch went from the bottom of the page up towards the dark blue mosaics of the star-scattered ceiling. He struggled to make out the family crest: four tiny birds in a four-pointed star-like shape. Where could it be? He looked around. A small comet in the wall put him on the right track. He went over and brushed it lightly with his hand. It moved. Farhad looked up again and noticed one star was suddenly shining particularly bright. He got up onto the table and pressed the star, triggering a sort of creaking mechanism that startled him. It revealed a small white casket inside an alcove, incrusted with stars and geometric patterns of exotic stones which echoed the designs of the vault. Farhad picked up the light chest and placed it on the table. It opened easily. But there was nothing inside.

Farhad rushed feverously back to the recess, only to find old parchments. Nader the Elder's heirs must have stored them all in there to protect them from possible thieves. Only the memoirs, too bulky to be hidden in the alcove, had remained on the table. He considered the curling parchments for a moment. The sheets were heavy and difficult to move. They were most likely full of legal documents enumerating the boundaries of his family's estates. When had the stone been moved? And why? Had it not been specified that it should never leave its hiding place? Who would have dared defy Farhad's ancestor?

He pulled himself together. Why was he letting himself get so frustrated? Had he not got what he came for? He walked back over to the memoirs and began to take photographs of each page of the manuscript, one by one. He was tempted to carry the whole book away, but he refrained in the hope that future generations of the family would one day find their way down there, into that magical place. And besides, taking the book out of the country was not an option as it would be instantly confiscated. He would be arrested for theft, as neither the memoirs nor any of the other contents of the house belonged to them now.

He checked the pictures were sharp and could be enlarged on his computer, then he put everything back as he had found it and left. Something told him he should not hang around. He stopped halfway up the steps. In his haste, he had forgotten to photograph the mosaics which he hoped to show his mother one day. He rushed out anyway, making sure to shut the trapdoor. He heard footsteps. Hachem had noticed his room was empty and was anxiously calling him from the garden.

'Mr Farhad… where are you?'

Hachem was already heading towards the barn, where the door was still wide open. Farhad came out into the moonlight with a smile.

'I'm here. I just stepped outside to get some air. I couldn't sleep… Every minute in this house is very precious to me. I wanted to make the most of it all; the heavens, the stars, the moon… You see?'

'I can understand that. But the night is cold and you have nothing but a shirt. Your hands are frozen. At least come and have a cup of tea in the kitchen.'

Hachem led him inside. They spent the remainder of the night talking about the past. When Farhad asked questions about the arrest of his grandfather, Hachem's eyes filled with sadness.

'They came for him in the middle of the night. It's been more than twenty years, but I remember it like it was yesterday. They waited for him downstairs. A guard came up and stood outside his bedroom. It gave me a turn to see all those people in the house. Your grandfather came down, dressed impeccably. He gave his wife a kiss, and she tried to give him a scarf, but he turned it down. 'It's no use, they won't let me keep it,' he said in his deep voice. 'He was acting impassive, determined to appear composed for his family's sake. Your father was there. He took him to one side and said a few words to him. The Pasdaran kept their distance, uneasy at disturbing your household in the middle of the night. Now they have all become so unbearably arrogant,' he confided, lowering his tone.

Until then this story had seemed abstract. That night, for the first time, Fahrad felt his father's grief, and he could appreciate how violently his family had been torn apart. The guards had intended to destroy them by removing the head of the clan, and they had succeeded.

'Did you ever find out what he said to my father?' Farhad asked.

'He never confided in me. I don't know, perhaps he urged him to continue practising medicine, for the sake of the Iranian people. Your father was never the same again, not even after you were born.'

Farhad nodded. His memories of his father were of a very stern man who rarely laughed.

'Your grandmother never recovered either. She lived for her family. But her life did go back to some semblance of normality, at least until your father's illness. Later, when I heard she wanted to leave the country with you both, I couldn't help being worried for her.'

Farhad reassured him. His grandmother had adapted well and had lived another ten years surrounded by old and more recent friends. In turn, Farhad asked Hachem about his life and news of his older children.

The next morning, Hachem insisted on cancelling the taxi reservation and driving Farhad to Tehran himself. On the way, Farhad was only half listening to Hachem, too lost in his own thoughts which were still fixated on the crypt and the stone. He had many questions he would have liked to ask him, given that the gardener had spent his whole life in the house, but it would have meant breaking his vow. Instead, he decided to concentrate on the memoirs. He hoped they would at least provide details about the lives of his gallant ancestors.

When they arrived in town, Farhad asked Hachem to drop him at the entrance to the bazaar.

'Why are you going to the bazaar?' Hachem asked. 'It is a dangerous place. You wouldn't have been dropped there in the old days.'

'But I was only six back then,' Farhad protested laughingly.

Hachem drove off as soon as Farhad tried to offer him money for petrol.

'I won't hear of it,' he said over and over as he climbed into the car.

Farhad thanked him and embraced him, wondering poignantly if their paths would ever cross again.

IV

For his research paper, Farhad had already organised a meeting with a merchant who was known for his active role in the revolution. Now, as he walked down one of the alleyways in the bazaar, he took in the new sights and sounds. It was lined with stall after stall, selling ancient glasswork, multi-coloured carpets, jewellery and embossed copper utensils. He stopped in front of a little table covered in red damask and pretended to take great interest in one of their samovars. That was the agreed signal.

'If that kind of item is to your taste, I have some vases that may interest you,' said the plump, bright-eyed merchant. 'Please come through.'

The merchant directed Farhad inside, then lowered the shutter halfway in one practised movement.

'The Revolutionary Guards are everywhere. The neighbours have a thousand eyes and a thousand ears,' he explained as he led Fahrad into his shop, an incongruous assortment of expensive furniture and knick-knacks.

His speech was marked by the typical drawling accent of the Gilan region, by the Caspian Sea.

'My offices are upstairs, but before we go up, I wanted to speak with you alone down here, without being interrupted by my staff.'

The merchant led them through a maze of small, rather cluttered rooms, to a larger one where he asked his visitor to wait a moment. Alone, Fahrad had a look around, then spent a few minutes playing with an amber rosary he found on a side table. He felt at ease sitting there, in this stranger's shop.

The merchant came back with a young servant who poured them tea.

'Welcome!' he said once they were alone, face to face. 'So, what brings you here?'

'I'm writing a report on the current situation of this country for an American geopolitical institute. I won't reveal my sources.'

'You will be searched when you leave the area,' the merchant said, his eyes fixed on the voice recorder.

'Our conversation will be encrypted.'

'All right. Go ahead.'

'Is the economic situation as bad as people make out?'

'The country is in bad shape. Inflation has been stuck at thirty per cent for some time now, and it is a drain on middle-class incomes. People can't make ends meet, life is very hard.'

'Weren't you, the bazaar merchants, the ones responsible for financing the revolution?'

'That's true. We were full of hope, but that hope was quickly shattered. We were on centre stage of the action.

In the first few hours of the revolution, men and women braved the curfew to go out and chant "God is great!" from the rooftops. I had just got married and we had decided to live in the centre of Tehran. My wife and I listened to them, hand in hand, and in that moment it seemed like we were part of something extraordinary. But the revolution soon descended into witch hunts, the like of which you cannot even imagine. Our neighbourhood was the scene of summary convictions; hangings and stonings took place on our doorstep, and gallows sprang up everywhere you looked.'

'Did no one rebel against this subversion of your revolution?' asked Farhad.

'The religious leaders hamstrung us with their carrot and stick tactics. I knew we'd lost the day I found out that thousands of Iranians believed they had seen Khomeini's face in the moon.'

Fahrad nodded, and the merchant went on: 'They've been in power for twenty-five years. They made a hundred billion dollars in the space of two years through the oil industry. Do you think they've distributed any of it to the people? No, they'd rather use it to help Hezbollah, or to invest in nuclear industries. If we complain, we are arrested.'

'Haven't there been any pockets of resistance?'

'Well, in 1999, some students tried to contest the government, but the demonstrations ended in a bloodbath. The new president has given us some cause for hope, but the number of arrests hasn't changed. You in the West for a while thought it was détente. Actually, that was not such

a bad thing, given how sorely we need you to lift your
sanctions in order to boost our economy.'

'How does the young generation fit into all this?' asked
Farhad.

'When they're not marching or taking drugs, they join
meditation circles. As far as the government is concerned,
it doesn't matter whether it's dope or meditation so long
as it keeps them out of politics. What is really horrific is
the execution of juvenile delinquents.' He went on: 'We
used to believe in a set of core values. We revolted for
them, and we ended up with a credulous society marked
by fear. Don't forget that amputation is still a legal pun-
ishment. Can you imagine a doctor coming to your home
and cutting off one of your family members' limbs in the
name of justice?'

By now, Farhad's stomach was churning, but the merchant was in full flow.

'It's not much better for young women. It is common
for wives to be repudiated the day after their wedding
night. Though their determination to change their lot
does mean women outnumber men in universities.'

Farhad had heard enough. As he was about to take
his leave, a thought came to him, and he decided to ask
straight out whether the merchant knew anything about
the Alamut stone.

'This is old news, but there is such a stone on sale at
Sotheby's in London. I saw the catalogue online. Do you
want to see what it looks like? Come with me, I'll show it
to you before you go.'

The merchant led Farhad through an animated alley of the bazaar and up some stairs. He was surprised to find a room quite sizeable and filled with ten or so employees all working on computers.

'Don't look so surprised. We work in import-export. You didn't think I earned a living selling bric-a-brac? That's just a hobby.'

He sat down in front of a computer and wheeled a desk chair forward with his foot. Convinced this would be the stone stolen from the crypt, Farhad could not contain his relief when he heard that this archaeological piece of Islamic art was still on sale.

He bent over to have a closer look at the full-page photograph of the stone; it was rough on one side and polished on the other.

'It's a meteorite fragment,' the merchant added. 'The tiny shining incrustations you see there are not pink diamonds, but chondrules, welded into the stone by the extreme heat. If you are interested, it is priced at eight hundred to a thousand pounds. Considering where it's supposed to have come from, that's a fair price.'

Farhad went on reading the catalogue entry. One of those stones had been taken to England by Lord Aspers at the end of the nineteenth century.

'A *pasdar* sold it on to an English merchant. I know, because he asked me for a quote. I can arrange for you to meet him, if you wish.'

Farhad was delighted to have uncovered a trail that might lead to his stone. The merchant noticed that his visitor seemed to be tempted by the offer, so he added with a nod, 'He is a measured, courteous man. You'll be pleasantly surprised.'

The merchant picked up the phone and dialled.

'Good morning, Mr Navidi. You may remember me, I'm the bazaar merchant you met a few months ago regarding a quote. I'm calling on behalf of a young researcher who is passing through and is looking for information on the Alamut stone. Would you be able to meet with him, preferably sooner rather than later?'

A meeting was arranged for the very same afternoon. Farhad thanked him sincerely. The merchant showed him to the door, and said, with an arm around his shoulder and his eyes brimming with emotion, 'Never forget, my son, that you are an Iranian. I hope that your report will paint a clear picture of this government's crimes.'

Once outside, Farhad had just made up his mind to extend his stay at the hotel when his phone started ringing. He frowned. It was a local call, but no one knew his number. He picked up and waited, without saying a word. A soft, singing voice spoke to him in Farsi. It was Parvine, one of his mother's cousins who still lived in their old district of Zafaranieh. She had heard he was in Tehran, and she wanted to invite him to tea at her house.

Caught off guard, but happy to hear from a family member, Farhad accepted.

In the meantime, he wandered around the bazaar to kill some time. The streets were noisy and the shops crammed full of customers. He treated himself to a chicken and cranberry kebab which he tucked into as he walked. He wanted to soak up as much of the city as he could, though it frustrated him to see the scaffolding for so many new buildings, which broke regulations, and which disfigured the city. He was outraged as he thought about those construction sites being open all night.

At three o'clock, he rang the bell of his cousin's gate. She praised him for coming back to his country as she led him into her home. They passed through two courtyards while she bombarded him with questions. Her loosely fitted dress swayed as she glided silently in her mules. Nowadays, her house was only a part of the large mansion they once owned, before it had been carved up in the revolution. The living room was decorated with traditional ornaments; a tarnished silver samovar and crystal candlesticks cut down to size adorned the fireplace. A low table was overflowing with Persian miniatures, medals, papier maché Russian boxes and a bowl filled to the brim with pistachios, dried figs and tiny translucent golden mulberries.

She led them both into the garden to rejoin her guests. Although much smaller than it once was, the garden had retained its majesty thanks to the grandeur of the trees. The winding path was lined by tall yews; the branches of a few young willows were swinging down over the pond. Her guests sat on wrought-iron chairs in the shade of the flat leaves of two Judas trees.

Farhad was astonished at how at ease they appeared to be. Although simply dressed, their movements and gestures

had retained a certain innate nobility. Some were talking
under the pergola while others had gathered around the
iron tables. Farhad was introduced. They greeted him
respectfully and asked after his family in Paris. A few of
them used to know his grandfather well and mentioned
the injustice of his arrest in the early days of the revolution. These people were relics of a lost world. They had
been the leaders of the country some thirty years ago, and
that experience allowed them to look back on events with
some perspective.

Farhad's host gestured for him to sit beside her. She
mentioned how, back in Paris, his mother worried about
him being in Tehran, which she considered one of the
most dangerous places in the world. Her first cousin had
tried to allay her fears by promising to get in touch with
him. Seeing her good nature, Farhad began to relax.

'Did you used to see much of my parents?' he asked.

'I did. What an interesting couple they were. Though
they had been born into traditional families, they both
had a progressive outlook on society. Your father chose to
work in a state hospital rather than have a private practice.
He made a point of treating all patients equally, and your
mother respected him for it.'

Farhad then discovered that his father had saved many
lives during the Iran-Iraq war. He had been a field doctor
before transferring to Tehran Hospital.

'Of course, your father got a terrible shock when a
patient he had just saved admitted to being your grandfather's executioner…'

This was said in passing, with an abrupt hand gesture as though she expected his approval, but she then fell silent as she saw Farhad's distressed expression.

'I thought you knew... You can imagine how unsettling it was for him. The gist of the story is that the executioner insisted out of gratitude that the Isfahan house be protected. But your father no longer wanted to live there anyway, so they offered it to Hachem instead.'

Conscious that his meeting was in less than an hour, Farhad got up to take his leave, while maintaining a neutral expression to conceal his emotions. A worried Parvine suggested he spend the night in her house.

'I'll show you around the places of your childhood,' she said.

Farhad was hesitant at first but, tempted by the thought of recapturing his childhood and waking up to the garden, he accepted the offer.

V

After closing the main gate behind him, Farhad got into the taxi, attempting to allay the worries that were eating away at him. He had little desire to meet a former Revolutionary Guard, especially in light of what he had learned about his grandfather.

To his surprise, the taxi stopped after a few minutes in front of the entrance to a Qadjar-style mansion. So, Mr Navidi, too, lived in an upmarket area. A major-domo opened the gate and waved the car in to park in front of the porch. As Farhad went to pay the fare, the driver made it seem as if he wished to decline, following the strict Persian etiquette that frowned upon crudely accepting the first offer of payment. Farhad walked around the great ornamental pond in the inner courtyard, and into the house. Soberly furnished, it had retained its historical feel. Time here seemed to have frozen at the end of the nineteenth century. He was ushered into the sitting room, where a replete man in Western clothing came over to greet him. Nothing about him seemed to suggest he was once one of the *pasdarans*, the Revolutionary Guards.

'Pleased to meet you.' The former guard was good-humoured and talkative, smoothly maintaining a flow of conversation as he led Farhad over to a corner of the sitting room.

'I trust you found the house without too much trouble?'

'I did, thank you.'

'Tehran was particularly congested tonight,' he said as he walked over to a serving tray. 'What would you prefer, tea or a cold drink? There's *sharbat*, if you're feeling the heat,' he added, as he held out a cup of tea.

Farhad politely accepted, and Navidi went on.

'The city has become so crammed. New buildings seem to spring up like mushrooms from one day to the next.'

Emboldened by his amicable host, Farhad was encouraged to speak openly. This man knew, of course, why the birth rate was soaring and why the city was being blighted by booming housing developments, but he prudently chose to stick to general remarks.

'I get the impression that a comfortable living is not easy to come by in this country. Why is it that the substantial oil revenues are not better distributed?'

'Ah, oil… Even such manna falls short of our country's needs, and besides, we don't have the means to refine it. You may not know this, but we even import our petrol… Although I have to agree that the choices made since the revolution have not always been the right ones,' he admitted, seeing Farhad's doubtful expression. 'Hundreds of opportunities have been missed. If we want to get the economy back on track, there are changes to be made.

The mullahs are unpopular enough as it is. We can only hope our more open-minded new president will be able to bring together the driving forces of this country.'

Perhaps thinking he'd said too much, he fell silent for a moment, and then changed the subject. 'I am proud to see that so many Iranians are doing so well abroad. Like yourself, just graduated from one of the top American universities, in the footsteps of a good number of our ministers before you. It is important for your compatriots to know that the door is open for them here. We want all those with American citizenship to come back and visit their homeland, so we can potentially encourage them to become dual citizens. I would be grateful if you could pass that message on.'

Unsure how to respond, Farhad punted for a more personal question. Mr Navidi readily offered a lengthy account of his career. 'I was one of the youngest Revolutionary Guards. During the Iran-Iraq war, I was entrusted with certain responsibilities and I rose up through the ranks. At the end of the war, I wanted to avoid joining the government. I had never been interested in politics. With hindsight, when you think of the mistakes made by our politicians over the last twenty years, you could say it was an error of judgement. I might have conceivably been able to prevent some of them, but I stand by my choices. When I was offered the opportunity to take over certain nationalised factories with the financial support of the *pasdarans*, I took it, and made a great success of it. But that's not how I made my fortune,' he added, with a self-congratulatory glance around the room. 'My real break came when I set up my own electronics business, which soon thrived.'

'That was quite a forward-thinking move, going into emerging technology.'

'Well, I was convinced that there was no reason why the Persians, with our great history of extremely complex arabesque designs in miniature painting and architecture, wouldn't be able to turn those talents to silicon chip circuits. It's been fifteen years now since I started the business and I take great pride in it.'

'Have you managed to export, too?'

'I have. Despite the restrictions, my products are sold across the Middle East. But enough about me. You come from a great Iranian family. How long is it since you left?'

'Eighteen years.'

'No wonder you feel it's all changed. I'm all for progress, but not at the expense of the finer things in life. Hence why I am restoring this house, bit by bit.' He led his guest into the next room. 'When I first bought it, the old owners had gone abroad and it had been looted. I decided to recreate each room. Renovating it has become a passion of mine. Your house, I'm sure, was even more magnificent. What do you think of this chandelier?'

Farhad answered with a fleeting smile. 'I'd only ever seen the old interiors in photographs, but I've just been to our house in Isfahan and it is all just as it was. And everything here, the chandelier, the wonderful Kashan carpets and the furniture, all seems perfectly in keeping to me.' He was being sincere.

'I have been well advised by the bazaar merchants,' Navidi said, 'but there's still much work to be done.'

Farhad who had not lost sight of the object of his visit decided this would be the opportune moment to bring up the stone. 'Actually, one of those merchants is the very reason I'm here. I am interested in the Alamut stone.'

'That talisman belonged to illustrious men. I had no plans to sell it, but an English dealer offered a good price. If you like, I can give you his contact details.'

Farhad knew that the amulet was already on sale at Sotheby's, but he accepted anyway. He was greatly disappointed to learn that Mr Navidi could offer no clues as to its whereabouts over the last nine hundred years.

As Farhad prepared to leave, his host offered to show him around the garden. 'There's something else you should see,' he said.

Farhad was beginning to feel a little weary, but he didn't want to be impolite. They went out through the large French windows at the back of the house and followed a path to a stone building. A surprise awaited him. There, a Volvo Coupe P1800 was carefully parked. From the layers of dust dulling the red paint on its bodywork, it was evident that it had never been used. 'I found it here when I bought the house,' he said, as Farhad walked around the car. 'It fitted in well with the place, so I kept it. Back when the previous owners were driving it, I would have been living up in the mountains with my family, a few sheep and no electricity. And now there it is, all old and rusty. Funny how these things turn out, isn't it?'

There was a pause, and it occurred to Farhad that this moment, this collision of past and present, would not be repeated. The former *pasdar* invited him to stay for dinner as he escorted him to the gate; Farhad courteously declined, explaining that his cousin was expecting him. The man nodded. Family was sacred.

'When do you fly back?' he asked.

'On Tuesday evening,' Farhad replied.

'Then I shall pass on instructions for them to spare you the formalities at the airport. I hope to see you back in your homeland, bringing the new generation along with you.'

As he left, Farhad felt his uneasiness return. The man had seemed nothing but civil and welcoming. How could he think him likeable after what he had learned about his grandfather's executioner? It seemed that the revolution had left Iranians essentially unchanged, and that they were not so different from the exiled diaspora.

Iran had been the first country to inaugurate an Islamic government. It would in all likelihood be the first to dispense with it. In spite of government rhetoric, most of the Iranians he had met were pro-Western. Would Iran one day go back to being an ally of the West? Farhad dearly hoped so, convinced as he was that his country would be crucial to peace in this powder keg of a region.

When he arrived at his cousin's house, Parvine had gone out and left him a note: his bedroom was on the first floor and his dinner was in the pantry. He had a quick snack and went up to his room. His bag was at the foot of the bed. He was so exhausted that, without even looking around him, he got undressed, slid into the cool sheets and fell asleep.

A gust of hot air awoke him the next morning. It took a few seconds for him to get his bearings. The sun was already high in the sky. It must have been at least ten o'clock. He went over to the window. The garden was bursting with life. Two chickadees were playing under the pergola, identifiable only by their black caps, which he could just pick out through the white jasmine. He breathed in the warm air. A pair of magpies were hopping about on the lawn, and a plump bumblebee was buzzing around in the shrubbery that reached up almost as high as his window. A heady fragrance wafted from the wisteria and tuberoses. He remembered how his grandmother never wanted their cuttings inside as the scent was too overpowering.

As the rays of sunlight continued to stream into his room, he moved away from his vantage point.

Parvine had left another note, with her office number should he need it. Otherwise she'd be back in the early afternoon. Farhad felt a little light-headed: he had the house all to himself.

He took some fruit from the kitchen and ambled cheerfully into the garden. He left his plate on a table under the Judas trees and began to stroll around. He decided to start at the bottom of the garden, following the yew-lined lane. It was a still day, but the shade from the trees would be pleasant. Then, after a moment's thought, he decided to cut across instead: as a child, he would not have followed the marked path. He would probably have tread barefoot across the grass. So he took off his shoes and headed towards the ornamental pond. He recalled how he used to watch the water boatmen jerkily skidding across the surface of this long stretch of water. He was glad to see the tadpoles were still there. Clearly nature did not care a fig about revolutions. Frogs and large gold-fish had lived side by side in Persia's ponds since time immemorial.

Under the midday sun, he felt rejuvenated. He went back to get his plate and sank down onto a deck chair. Iran's sun-ripened fruit had an exceptional flavour. As he sat there, it came to him that he needed to book his flight to London.

Over the next three days, Parvine took him on a tour of his past. She planned the itinerary carefully, and they took their time in every spot. Seeing his family's houses, he was deeply struck by the thought of the lives they had lost. His mother had never mentioned the property they had been dispossessed of.

By his last day, one question was still bugging him.

'Why did my father choose to stay after the revolution, given what had happened to my grandfather?' he asked.

'Your father was an idealist,' she replied. 'He knew his country needed doctors. War broke out quite quickly after the revolution, and his purpose was to cure the sick and relieve their pain. He thought that in so doing he would be building a better society, but it didn't work out that way.'

'How did he find out that he had treated my grandfather's executioner?'

'From the man himself. He admitted it once he had been cured. They say he apologised profusely and even offered to make him Minister for Health, but your father refused. He kept his integrity and said that he would have cared for him, whoever he was. For him, the Hippocratic Oath went beyond family matters.'

Farhad took pride in learning that his father had been faithful to his principles despite what he'd gone through. Meanwhile, as he observed Parvine, he realised that she was stuck in the past. By now, he was keen to leave. He would return home with the memoirs of his ancestor Nader, and he had learned that nothing was ever black or white. In Iran, life went on, of course, more uncomfortable and more dangerous than before, but Iranian people got on with it. Some were even happy.

As for him, his life lay elsewhere.

VI

Once in London, Farhad checked into a modest bed and breakfast in Earl's Court. He hardly knew the city. The English, like the Americans, tended to be friendly and obliging towards strangers, which made a great difference to his day-to-day life. There were many other foreigners in the same neighbourhood, but they all seemed to live in their own little bubbles.

He was still reeling from the visit back to his homeland, and at times those thoughts would take over and leave him feeling rather dispirited. His mind constantly returned to his father who, Farhad admitted to himself, was too absorbed by war and his illness to leave much time for his son. It must have been a trial for his mother to see that even the birth of their little boy couldn't free her husband from his melancholy. At that thought, an aching knot tightened at the pit of his stomach. It was then that he understood that his general malaise could not be attributed entirely to exile.

Farhad had been exposed to the new face of Iran with all its complexities and paradoxes. At Yale, when he had met young Iranian students full of enthusiasm for the current regime, he had made a point of avoiding them. But meeting *pasdar* Navidi had tempered his convictions.

Now he realised that his attachment to Iran was both an anchor and a hindrance in his life. The Isfahan garden could no longer be his point of reference. Henceforth, he had a choice between either feeling out of place everywhere or endeavouring to feel at home anywhere.

It took him a few days to pull himself together. After all, he came from a family who knew how to pick its battles. The thought that he would always be torn between the present and his Persian past no longer troubled him. Bolstered by his dual heritage he accepted that he must move forward and put his mind to other things. Coming to terms with this gave him new and unexpected energy.

He decided to get on with researching his paper while waiting for the day the stone would be sold. His top-floor room overlooked some trees and was bathed in full sunlight. He worked on his computer and made calls sitting on a sofa under an open window.

Before long, he had almost forgotten he was on foreign turf. Upon his arrival, he had contacted the Dean of the Yale Global Institute for International Affairs, who had asked him to include extremist activities in British Muslim communities in his report. An official letter outlining his tasks had confirmed his extended mission.

Farhad then got in touch with officers at Scotland Yard who advised him to begin by reading *Architect of Global*

Jihad by Abu Musab, a jihadist and opponent of hierarchical organisations who advocated decentralisation in the global war, and had been captured by the Americans. He found the text online and took the time to read all one thousand six hundred and four pages. The theoretician's ideas intrigued him.

The Dean of Yale also managed to arrange an interview for him with a former Director of the Secret Services, who described the role of certain mosques and charitable organisations in the proliferation of terrorism.

To further his enquiries, he went to the library at Chatham House, the Royal Institute for International Affairs, where he found a list of associations suspected of promoting radical Islam. One name immediately struck him: Al Rhubni. Hadn't Reza travelled to London expressly to work for that very organisation? He took the name down and went outside to call Mr Dalavandi. Reza's uncle confirmed that it was indeed the association where his nephew worked as treasurer. His heart skipped a beat. Was Reza inadvertently being used as a puppet for a terrorist cell?

He went back to Scotland Yard in a state of bewilderment. Sergeant William McGuire received him warmly, keeping in mind that he came highly recommended by a prestigious American university. Farhad cut to the chase. 'I need to pick your brain. Have you heard of the Al Rhubni Foundation?'

'Yes, in fact it is under close surveillance. It is suspected of using charity work as a front for funding extremist activity, and perhaps terrorism. If this is confirmed by our investigation, it won't be long before they're subject to a police raid. Between you and me, we are going to have to do the same for many trusts in the coming months. For now, Al Rhubni is certainly on Scotland Yard's radar.'

Coming away from the meeting, a deeply troubled Farhad could think only of Reza.

A graduate of Wharton Business School, Reza could have secured a high-flying job in any bank. But that had never interested him. There had always been a humanitarian side to Reza which Farhad secretly admired. He had chosen finance not for personal gain, but in order to help solve economic crises and offset their alarming impact on social destabilisation. 'The world,' he would say, 'watched powerlessly from the sidelines as the middle classes in developed countries were gradually stripped back.' According to him, that was a prime cause of political instability and a driving force of extremism. He had always taken that line, even back when they were teenagers. His mission as an adult, he used to say, would be to anticipate such crises and find economic solutions. As soon as he had graduated, he tried to find a position in an international organisation such as the World Bank, but he was consistently turned down. So he moved away from that sector, to become treasurer of the Al Rhubni Foundation.

'He is obviously in the dark about all this,' Farhad said to himself, shaking his head. But how was he supposed to break this news to him? They had grown up and gone to school together, so Farhad knew Reza's idiosyncrasies, his strengths and flaws, all too well. Reza was incredibly proud and struggled to accept criticism. Farhad knew that this news would put a strain on their friendship. Nonetheless, there was no putting it off.

When he returned to his room that night, he decided to give himself a bit of a breather. He had just got his ancestor's memoirs printed and he was transported to another world from the opening lines. Nader the Elder denounced his contemporaries' credulity and showed how the man who had once been his childhood friend had, through his reading, reinvented himself and become unrecognisable.

By a subtle mixture of charm and force, Hassan Sabah supervised the recruitment and indoctrination of his accomplices, chosen for their youth and physical strength. For instance, Nader wrote of a magical garden that Hassan had created in the fortress. He would drug the young men with hashish and, once they had fallen sound asleep, he would have them taken to the secret garden of trickling streams and voluptuous young women. When they awoke, the young men were met with unimaginable pleasures in what they believed to be the Gardens of Paradise, as promised in the Quran. Nader noted in passing that the word 'paradise' came from the ancient Persian word *Pairidaeza*, or 'garden'.

After several days, they were given a second hashish drink before they were brought before Hassan Sabbah, to tell him that they had been to Paradise. Then Hassan had them led through seven stages. Before they were admitted into the sect they underwent intensive physical and intellectual training. In the final stage, they had to master several languages. Isolated and cut off from their families, they became fearless machines with a single purpose: to die in combat.

Farhad put his book down, deep in thought. Any parallel with modern terrorists seemed tenuous. Here was a man who locked his recruits into a strict hierarchy with an aim to target the rich and famous, viziers, kings and sultans. By contrast, today's atrocities were committed against civilians by disparate groups of disillusioned men and women with no direct connection to the cause they defended. Though they were sometimes following strict orders, more often than not they acted alone or in small groups. Only if they were successful would some terrorist organisation then lay claim to their actions.

Farhad carried on reading late into the night, intrigued by the description of the order's hierarchy. Under the imam, the 'Grand Master of the mountain', were the *Dais*, a group of well-versed individuals whose mission was to visit cities, where they would preach and recruit novices. Then there were the *Rafiqs*, also partly initiated, who were in charge of the building and protection of fortresses.

The *Fidays*, or 'the devoted', acted as executioners. Often from poor backgrounds, they received a first-rate education that encompassed languages, science, philosophy and the *batin*; as well as espionage training in the art of disguise and dissimulation in order to get close to their target.

Farhad paused once again. The *Fidays* had been much discussed throughout history. They had terrorised the Muslim world and beyond for two centuries. But how far-reaching had their activities actually been? They hadn't altered the course of history. So what impact would modern terrorists have, even if they continued to sow terror through cities, and even if an increase in the number of attacks was to be expected? Quite limited, in the end.

Farhad made up his mind to call Reza the next morning, and they agreed to meet at midday in the Tate Modern.

Farhad got there first. There were not many visitors in the hall, the great 1930s factory that had been converted into a museum.

He was gazing up at Louise Bourgeois's huge bronze spider hanging from the ceiling when he spotted his friend's slender outline coming towards him. They were both so delighted to see each other that Farhad lost his train of thought. The two friends took the escalator up to the Rothko exhibition.

'You look great!' Reza exclaimed.

'It's all that Iranian sunshine,' Farhad replied.

'Go on, tell me about your trip.'

'At the beginning, I was happy to be back among the trees, the mild air, the colours… I felt really good. But once I started digging a bit and hearing people's stories, I was anxious to get away.'

Reza nodded gravely. He too had thought about going

back to Iran when he had been unable to find work in Paris, but he had decided against it for the same reasons.

As they walked into the first exhibition rooms, deserted at that time of day, Reza asked Farhad what he was doing in London.

'I've been asked to do some research into terrorist networks. You'll have a shock when you hear what I found out. The name of your foundation appears in one of the confidential lists.' He spoke slowly, almost in a whisper.

'What are you talking about?' Reza exclaimed. His voice echoed through the empty rooms.

'Someone named Al-Khuri is, according to my sources, one of your foundation's main donors. He is suspected of being behind the attacks that were foiled last winter.'

Farhad could tell by his slight shudder that Reza had heard that name before.

'Since those failed attacks, the British authorities have disbanded organisations, frozen bank accounts and arrested imams. You should also know that Scotland Yard have a file on your charity, and it is under investigation. You can expect a police raid in the coming weeks. But don't go spreading this around.'

They kept walking past the vibrant Rothko paintings.

Farhad went on, his hands behind his back, 'I'm telling you all this because I wanted you to know they are using your integrity as a cover. You're part of their window dressing.'

Reza stopped dead in his tracks. Petrified, he exclaimed: 'I had no idea, in case you're wondering! And anyway, how do you know all this? You've only just got here!'

He bolted out of the room just as a group of students came in. Farhad was kicking himself. Why hadn't he been a bit more tactful in bringing it up? Wouldn't it have been better to have kept this to himself? What if Reza decided to take his own life? Appalled at this thought, Farhad punched the palm of his hand. The guard looked up at the smacking sound, surprised to see such aggression in front of the American artist's tranquil and meditative work. Farhad paced up and down the middle of the gallery. He didn't see Reza coming back in, and he jumped when he heard his voice. 'Alarm bells should have been ringing when the interviews went so well. I'll have to resign, it's as simple as that.'

While his friend was talking, Farhad tried to pull himself together. Reza couldn't be rushed. Farhad apologised for his abruptness and suggested they get some lunch. He took him by the arm and led him out of the exhibition. They went to the cafeteria on the same floor and sat down in front of a bay window overlooking the Thames. With an impenetrable expression, Reza gazed down over London, which was shrouded in a sheet of grey from the City to St Paul's Cathedral. Even though they weren't hungry, they ordered two soups; pea with mint, and carrot and coriander.

Farhad spoke first. 'My friend, you don't have to convince me that you didn't know anything about the foundation's activities. I wasn't even sure at first whether I should say anything. More likely than not, Scotland Yard will decide not to act and will leave the foundation alone so they can keep an eye on it and catch as many people as they can. Actually, that's why I had to tell you. You can't resign, you have to stay where you are. There might be plots in the pipeline. Your help will be needed.'

'If you're asking me to spy on my colleagues for the Brits,' Reza responded hotly, 'you've got another thing coming! Are you forgetting how two-faced they are, with all their calculated attempts to weaken Iran? Do you really want me to help them out?'

Farhad paused for a moment to collect his thoughts, then he spoke measuredly.

'I understand your anger. The British have acted poorly. They have made many mistakes in the Middle East, but they aren't the only colonisers. You have to look past that and help immigrant families make a new start here. And what kind of message will it send if we let terrorists have their way?'

'That those accountable should pay, for instance,' Reza murmured under his breath.

'Accountable for what, exactly?' Farhad objected. 'You are talking about injustices committed decades ago. And even if you had the people really responsible right here in front of you, what would you do? Stick a knife into them? It's not worthy of people like us.'

Reza stared down at his plate.

'They're still involved in operations as we speak, dropping bombs and killing whole families,' Reza replied. 'They call it "collateral damage". And you want me to take their side?'

'War is always horrific. But bringing the fight here is not the answer.'

There was a pause and Farhad began to think he'd gained some ground. To prove to Reza there were no hard feelings, he started telling him about his search for the memoirs of Nader the Elder, his descent into the crypt and the story of the Alamut stone. Reza's eyes widened. He was carried back eighteen years to the garden in Isfahan among the fruit trees. Countless times they had played detectives or done treasure hunts there, and they'd never dreamed there would be a crypt right beneath their feet. Farhad then described how their old Tehran district had changed.

'Your house has been made into flats and mine has been split into two. It's all very bizarre.'

They sat in silence for a moment, thinking back to the lost paradise of their childhood. Then Farhad told him about the stone's disappearance and his hope of buying it back. Reza too was eager to read the memoirs and to see the stone once it was retrieved.

'It's getting late. I should get back to the office,' Reza announced, glancing at the big clock.

'No problem. I'll get the bill,' said Farhad.

Farhad watched his friend leave, feeling rather perplexed.

He went back down the escalator and crossed the metal suspension bridge over the Thames. He didn't notice the drizzle on his face but he was careful not to skid on the slippery skywalk. He was frustrated with himself. Why hadn't he thought of arranging another meeting with Reza? He knew that if he persuaded Reza to spy on the foundation, he would be putting him at great risk.

'The more we can put it off, the better,' he murmured as he quickened his pace.

He was more troubled by the last two hours than he cared to admit. He asked himself what he was doing in this city. What had brought him here, against his mother's wishes, only to risk quarrelling with his closest friend?

Then the main reason for his trip to London came back to him. The stone would be sold in a few days' time. As he stepped down into Blackfriars Underground station he promised himself he would finish his report as soon as possible.

Back at the hotel he had a sudden burst of energy. He got changed to go jogging in Hyde Park.

He took the bridle path and was hardly out of breath when he reached the Serpentine, so he decided to keep going towards Kensington Palace. As he ran, he could feel his tense muscles easing. The season was nearing its end and the maple trees had turned purple. His rubber soles crackled their way through the dead leaves, and his nostrils flared at the slightly acidic smell of autumn's carpet. On his way back, he strolled down Queen's Gate, calmer now.

VII

Farhad slept badly that night and decided not to make any reference to Reza's foundation in his report. He would run the risk of drawing attention to that association with no way of getting his friend out of the hornet's nest. Yet describing the role of various charitable foundations in London seemed to him to be an essential part of his investigation. So he chose instead to approach it from the angle of privately financed mosques, starting by paying them a visit.

The first on his list was Finsbury Park, famous since Abu Hamza, the dangerous preacher, had been found guilty and put away for inciting terrorism. Farhad was astonished to find it was a brick building, several storeys high. What a contrast with the superb turquoise-tiled mosques of Isfahan, Samarkand or South Pakistan.

'How could they have allowed such a monstrosity?' Farhad exclaimed as he gazed at the mosque from the opposite side of the road.

He often spoke out loud when he was particularly outraged. To his great surprise, he heard a voice behind him answer, 'You are quite right, but you have to understand it's all part of a deal struck with the West.'

Farhad turned around. That perfect English accent belonged to an old man, clearly a product of the melting pot of the British Commonwealth, in an old raincoat far too big for him.

He went on: 'The gap between rich and poor in this country is widening. The middle class is slowly disappearing. Immigrants are feeling the effects of the crisis, just like everyone else. We live in poverty without any prospect of change. They thought they could make it all go away just by building a few mosques. But now for the first time, our young people are at a loose end. Many of them are ready to do anything to make something of themselves.'

'Like what?' asked Farhad.

'Like blowing themselves up for a cause or joining foreign fighters,' he answered. 'They're never the same when they come back.'

He went on explaining his frustrations for a while. Farhad thanked him, and asked for his name and address in case he needed to cite his contribution in the report, then watched him limp away.

He stood outside reflecting for a few minutes before going into the building. Inside, it resembled a 1960s primary school. It was empty save for a few veiled women chatting among themselves. He decided against interrupting them. With nothing else to do, he walked towards the Underground to get back home quickly. He needed to push forward on writing up his report so he could send it off to Yale.

Friday being the most important day in Islam, he set it aside for Regent's Park Mosque.

In the meantime, Farhad got in touch with different communities in the north of England, where he had heard tensions were running high. In order to be well received, he didn't mention his investigation, instead introducing himself as a postgraduate student who was writing a thesis about the opportunities for Muslim immigrants to integrate in different European countries.

After a few setbacks, doors started to open when he name-dropped his university. A Pakistani doctor from Saint Luke's Hospital in Bradford agreed to meet him the next day.

Farhad caught a morning train.

He arrived early and decided to take a walk around before going to his meeting. He wanted to find out as much as possible about that town where it was said communities lived side by side without much interaction and also where a radical struggle was brewing among the new immigrants.

After a few steps, he felt he could have been in a mini-Islamabad. Veiled women strolled alongside their children in school uniforms. Past small grocery shops overflowing with fruit and vegetables, he came to shop windows full of vibrantly coloured clothes. With every step, it reminded him more and more of the Middle East. He came to a stop in front of a box of fresh okra which he had only ever seen in Iran. Afghan merchants, easily recognisable

by their square woollen hats, sat on the pavement selling
pirated films. Recognising features similar to some of his
fellow Iranians, if slightly more austere, Farhad asked
them the way to Western Road in Farsi. They directed
him to the right, hardly surprised that he spoke to them
in their own language. A jeweller was standing outside his
store, piled up with Indian-style bracelets studded with
diamonds and Balash rubies, inviting his regulars in. A
little further on, Farhad came across a quieter street of
shabby stucco, where he felt he was back in England. He
stopped in front of No. 7 and rang the bell.

The Pakistani doctor stepped back to let him in then
locked the door. He showed him into a living room that
led out onto a rather dark patio. On a low white wood
table, the man had prepared strong Darjeeling tea, just
the way they drank it back home. He seemed ill at ease
as if he was already regretting agreeing to meet him. To
avoid any suspicion surrounding their appointment he
had told his colleagues that he was seeing one of his wife's
cousins that afternoon. Farhad understood; he did not
want to cause the man any trouble.

This family man listened carefully to the first question
and gave a very honest answer. Just like his neighbours,
he was indeed advised by the people from the mosque
– advice he described as pointed – as to how he should
run his household, how to respect Ramadan, and how to
dress his daughters, including that they should wear the
veil from puberty onwards. He and his wife had not given
in to pressure. But there were underlying threats. Both

of them worked at the hospital, but their salaries barely covered their mortgage payments. People had made offers on their house, but they were reluctant to leave the area, despite the fact that they had been called bad Muslims by neighbours. They always went to Friday prayers, wanting to remain a part of the community, but the situation was getting harder. More and more friends who had been taken in by powerful influences were shunning them.

Farhad asked how he had the energy to resist. The poor man's jaw tightened as he revealed how, during one sermon, an imam had encouraged the congregation to ensure that their Muslim neighbours respected the precepts as set out by the mosque, adding that those who did not comply would be denounced as apostates. From that day on, the doctor had realised that those imams didn't have religion, but indoctrination, in mind. The British government had allowed the financing of their places of worship through private Qatari and Saudi funds. Even the imams' studies had been provided for.

Surprised, Farhad wondered if all of this was verifiable. The doctor leaned towards him to explain how a discreet attendant kept an eye on the mosque every day to make sure that the fundamentalist tradition was being preached. Only the imam knew about this warden who reported back to foreign benefactors.

'Wahhabism, one of the most conservative interpretations of Islam, didn't exist until the end of the 18th century. The prophet Mohammad was very open-minded. Didn't he stipulate in the Medina constitution that Muslims,

Christians, Jews and even Pagans had equal political and cultural rights?'

Farhad felt a surge of sympathy for this courageous and cultured man who had dared speak to him so openly. That day, Farhad realised that only a better understanding of the holy books and of the different branches of Islam would enable many of the faithful to resist fundamentalism. He took his leave, feeling a wave of anger building inside him. He was appalled at the amount of pressure the imams had to withstand. How was it possible that, in a Western city, preachers could be spied upon by foreign agents who threatened their livelihoods if they did not deliver a particular message?

On his way home, Farhad thought about the damage that some imams were causing. As he walked back, those identical houses came to symbolise the lives of the decent, uprooted families who occupied them. He pictured the challenges they faced in adapting to the climate and local customs, compounded by the continuous pressure to return to their roots, which dissuaded them from integrating for fear of cutting ties with their communities. The exploitation of this confusion was so overt. This meeting had allowed him to grasp the tangible reality of these fears. He tried not to let anxiety overwhelm him. On the Underground, Farhad found himself among a group of Pakistani passengers and noted the gentle, uncomplaining look on their faces. Their eyes lowered when his gaze became insistent. He wanted to shake these people and tell them how vital it was to fight against the invisible enemy who was destroying the lives of future generations. He wished he could speak out in the train, to warn them, but he restrained himself.

Back at his flat, he added a detailed report on his conversation with the doctor to his article. He concentrated on showing how Wahhabism, just one of the many branches of Islam, was in danger of dominating sermons in British mosques. He advocated a greater monitoring of the financing of mosques, which were run off gas and oil funds. He suggested promoting increased pluralism in religious teachings in mosques, madrasas and Koranic schools.

VIII

Farhad had not lost sight of the main reason he was in London, and on the day the stone was to be unveiled he was the first at Sotheby's to hold lot number 188 in his hand. The stone was incrusted with sparkling shards, just like pink diamonds. He picked up a magnifying glass from the table to take a closer look at the surface, which was soft and polished on one side, rough on the other. The stone consisted of millions of agglomerated granules. His breath was taken away. He was dazzled by one of the glistening fragments. Even with the naked eye, it was extraordinarily bright. Farhad felt the weight of the stone in his hand. He assumed from its density that it was indeed a meteorite. He recalled how, in geology class, he had learned that when asteroids eventually fall to earth, after millions of years of floating in space, they fuse and considerably diminish in size on entering the Earth's atmosphere. Some meteorites cool by just one degree over a million years, which would explain how they accumulate crystals and semi-precious stones. Farhad could see those gems best on the unpolished side of the fracture.

With the stone in his hand, he read the catalogue entry 'Mineral asteroid with pink peridot incrustations'. To his surprise, the catalogue mentioned that it had once belonged to the founder of a Persian sect, as was confirmed by a small inscription in Farsi on the polished side. The asteroid was estimated at £800. He could certainly understand people's fascination with it. He closed his eyes to process all the emotions that it roused in him. To think it had remained locked in his ancestors' crypt for so long! Did it have powers, as some claimed? He turned to speak to the young sales expert.

'Is this stone definitely authentic?'

'Its composition, along with these inscriptions, leave little doubt. But its value is purely symbolic,' he answered.

Farhad asked if he could have the name of the seller once he had bought it. The sales expert was very apologetic, but house regulations would not allow that. No exceptions.

Farhad was unperturbed.

He was convinced that he was holding his family stone in his hands. And since his own suitcase had not been searched on Mr Navidi's orders, he didn't wonder at how it could have left Iran. He was not best pleased at the prospect of paying £800 for the privilege of reclaiming something that belonged to him. He certainly did not want to exceed the base estimate, so he put down a bid of £850. As he left, he glanced absentmindedly around at the sophisticated women who were examining Safavid ceramics.

In the interim, Farhad's life returned to normal. He was determined to put the stone out of his mind until the day of the sale. He carried on with his investigations, gathering conclusions for his report.

Reading the memoirs was his anchor point every evening. The pages inspired him to persevere with his painstaking work, as if the text had opened up a line of communication between himself and Nader the Elder, ten centuries on. There was magic at work, the very magic his great-aunt had talked about. She had sensed that he would need this exchange more than anyone else in his family.

Thanks to the book's companionship, Farhad settled easily into his solitude. His only contact with the outside world was through the occasional long, late-night call with his friends in Paris. Nobody mentioned Reza; with the exception of Bardia, none of them knew that he was in London. Farhad took great care not to pour salt into the wound caused by Reza's silence. In the first few days after their lunch at the Tate, his heart had leapt every time the telephone rang, only to have sunk once he heard the voices of his mother or his friends at the other end of the line. Although he was resigned to Reza's long silence, he still refused to believe that his old friend had drifted to what he had started to call the 'other camp'.

A few weeks had gone by when Farhad decided to get back in touch with Reza. They agreed to go for a walk together in Hyde Park that Saturday morning.

At the park, Reza seemed on edge.

'Do you see that horde?' Reza remarked as they walked past Speaker's Corner. 'Westerners bring hostility upon themselves with their foreign intrusions.'

'What makes you think you're some great righter of wrongs?' Farhad retorted.

'What about you, hiding behind your papers and your scribbling, and thinking that's the way to change the world!'

'Sure, helping people to integrate into a new country is less sensational than playing the martyr and plotting stunts,' cried Farhad, indignant that his life choices were under fire.

'I have to admit there's something quite fascinating about being able to choose the time of your own death. And perhaps even the deaths of others, too,' Reza replied.

'It's against our religion, and you know it,' stuttered an alarmed Farhad.

His world was falling apart. He was left tongue-tied as his friend carried on unleashing a nonsensical tirade.

'The kind of life on offer here doesn't appeal to everyone,' Reza went on. 'Besides, what can we aspire to in the West? Going to the supermarket more often? A few more Starbucks coffees? Some Muslims settle for that life. They resign themselves to it once they have children. But others have reservations. Why do you think so many of them want to engage in jihad instead? I have a certain respect for their decision, even if I don't think I'd be brave enough to enrol.'

'If you don't endorse the world we live in, you should fight to make it a better place,' Farhad retorted. 'Help people settle in here. Give them a purpose in life, instead of leading them astray. Believe me: any contribution, even passive, to the murder of innocent civilians will do nothing to help your cause. Think of future generations who will have to pay the price for these fundamentalist brutes. We will all be hated because of them and their attacks. That's exactly what they want, to create divisions within Western societies. Changing the course of history as it happens, that's true heroism. You should reread Camus's *The Rebel*, that might help you see things more clearly.'

'Thank you, Herr Professor!' sneered Reza.

'I feel as if I don't know you anymore,' Farhad despaired, shaking his head. They stood stock still, face to face. Farhad stared straight into his eyes, trying to figure him out. But Reza turned away to avoid his gaze.

'I need more time,' he said with a dismissive gesture.

It was with a heavy heart that Farhad nodded and watched his friend walk away.

IX

In spite of his concerns about Reza, Farhad stuck to his schedule and visited Regent's Park Mosque that Friday evening at five o'clock, as planned. When he arrived, worshippers were coming and going. The ceiling of the prayer room was adorned by two grand crystal chandeliers. Aside from those distinct signs of Western influence, to Farhad the mosque could not have been more exotic. He went into the bookshop, with its enormous glass window looking out onto the entrance hall, and began browsing the books. Several titles caught his eye. He was surprised to find them here. He picked out a few, along with some philosophical works and a private prayer book while he was at it, then headed over to the till. When the cashier saw this selection, he looked up with keen eyes, flicking back and forth between Farhad's face and the books. Two of the texts were about the Medina period, and both were emphatic endorsements of jihad. After he had paid, the curious cashier invited him along to a meeting that was about to take place in an adjoining room.

Farhad accepted, only too happy to have an excuse to

stick around and observe the congregation. Like most mosques in Britain, the doors of this place of worship were open to both branches of Islam. Had it not taken many centuries, Farhad thought to himself, for Catholics, Protestants and Baptists to learn to live together in harmony? Although the gaping global rift between Sunnites and Shiites was being wrenched ever wider by radicals on both sides, time would surely heal the wound.

The bookseller lowered the steel shutters of his shop with a clang and came over to inform Farhad that the meeting was about to begin. He clearly took pride in holding the keys to the premises. He showed his customer into a large circular room where the congregation was already seated. Farhad was struck by the respectful hush that had descended here. Two imams sat down beside a lectern on a raised platform. He hadn't noticed them come in. The dark shade of their eyes and beards contrasted starkly with their pale skin. One of them took the floor.

'Brothers, welcome to your sacred house! You are residents of a foreign land. Let us preach the message of our great religion to this land. Think of yourselves as envoys. You must be exemplary in your obedience to the laws of the Holy Book. Prayers alone are not enough. You must serve the faith in everything you do. Those who choose the easy path and blend in will become accomplices to Western unbelievers. Let your conscience be your guide. Apostates will feel our wrath.'

As the imam's invective went on, he warned that those who integrated would become second-class citizens, passively taken in by Western decadence. He urged them to be disciplined and practising at all times. At the end of this emphatic speech, he asked if there were any questions.

Silence. No one dared speak. Farhad stood up impulsively and asked, 'Why stand in the way of religion and integration? No one is stopping Muslims in the West from praying or going to the mosque. Rather than railing against this country, shouldn't we instead be grateful to have been welcomed into a place where we can practise our religion, where we can give our children an education fit to make them citizens of the future? Why should seventh-century laws be applicable to the countries we are obliged to live in?'

Farhad looked around him, only to be faced with expressions of unease and incomprehension. The imam took advantage of this pause to pick up where he had left off as if there had been no interruption. Farhad sat back down. The whole congregation turned their heads and their attention enthusiastically back to the lectern. Glad to continue without responding to this intruder, they trustingly let themselves be swept along once again by the preacher's skilful rhetoric.

Resolved to get away as quickly as possible, Farhad was one of the first to leave. He stormed off, chastising himself. How could he have been so impulsive as to speak without any preparation, thus exposing his convictions to such a hostile audience? A slim young man of about average height caught up with him. He must have been around twenty years old and was wearing jeans and a jacket. He warmly praised Farhad's speech. But a sullen Farhad marched on towards Baker Street station, taking no notice of the persistent voice behind him until they reached the Underground escalators.

'Why are you pestering me?' he eventually demanded as he turned to face the young man.

'Because this is the first time that I have met someone brave enough to stand up to the imams. You see, Islam has been exploited for political ends through the centuries. In the words of Khomeini, "Islam is politics or it is nothing." Therein lies the ambiguity.'

That quotation caught Farhad's attention. Once they were in the tube carriage, Farhad let the persistent young man sit next to him.

'Look,' he continued, 'spiritual leaders know how to debate. The theological studies to become an imam are long and exacting. They can take up to ten years, and rhetoric is a key pillar of the course. You stood no chance against them,' he concluded with a smile.

The young man introduced himself. His name was Karim Suleimani and he was finishing a doctorate in theology. He couldn't agree more with Farhad: peaceful co-existence was possible. Past centuries proved it. Islam had existed for thirteen hundred years, and never before had it faced the problems of today. Karim's voice carried over the noise of the train. He used the example of the *dhimmis*, foreigners who had been tolerated, sometimes even welcomed, on Islamic soil. He outlined the need for Muslims to follow suit and adapt to the West. The tube journey went by quickly, although it was fifteen stations long. They carried on talking as they got out onto the platform and went up the escalator.

Before they went their separate ways, Karim invited Farhad to a panel discussion in Oxford the following Tuesday. They could meet inside Karim's college.

'There will be excellent professors on the subject, and it starts at five p.m. You won't be disappointed,' he called out as he left. 'And if you like, you can stay for dinner at the High Table – a privilege reserved for postgrads.'

Farhad, who was well aware of the unique honour of being invited to dine at the dons' table of an Oxford college, hesitated only momentarily before accepting.

Back at his flat, Farhad got out Niffari's *Book of Stations*, which he had bought at the mosque. He discovered that this great poet had been persecuted for his mysticism because it challenged the precepts of Islam. So it seemed conservative fanatics who stood in the way of other Islamic groups were nothing new. Farhad dropped off to sleep with the thought that these days the real danger was not merely the persecutions of mystics, but mass indoctrination by the ultra-conservative Wahhabis. His experience that day had been a prime example.

Farhad decided to shut himself in over the weekend so he could polish off his report. By the time he closed down his computer, happy with his work, it was six o'clock on Sunday evening. In a rather audacious conclusion, he warned that if nothing was done to counteract the first stages of radicalisation, Western societies would be at great

risk, as their freedom of thought and religion left them
vulnerable. In his memoirs, Farhad's ancestor had wondered how a handful of uncivilised men had managed to
convert all of Persia. Now Farhad asked himself whether
the same tragedy was about to unfold in the Western
world. It had taken three centuries for Persia to usher in
the more liberal Islam that had flourished in the tenth
and eleventh centuries, the time of Nader the Elder. He
recommended promoting other more enlightened readings of Islam, to undermine any perversions of the faith.

Over the last few days, Farhad had ordered two takeaway pizzas, and the empty boxes were scattered around
his kitchen. He had a shower, got changed and went out.
In the distance he could see strips of red brake-lights
from the weekend traffic jams. What difference was there
between his life and the lives of English people his age?
Not all of them were free from prejudice. He could sometimes feel their hostile gaze, but he could put himself in
their shoes. In many London boroughs the English had
become a minority. The city was now a megalopolis, and
it wasn't theirs anymore.

Lost in thought, he had walked quite a distance and
by now was strolling through Chelsea neighbourhoods.
Here, he was again in traditional Britain. Families were
unpacking their cars, back home from the country. He
observed this affluent, privileged world from a distance.
Then he remembered that he had had no news from the
outside world for days, and on his way home, he went
into a shop to pick up a copy of the *Sunday Times*. The

Pakistani owner tentatively tried to spark up a conversation. Farhad listened to him politely. He had been in London for years. A nuclear civil engineer, he had been forced to leave his home country when he got into trouble with the government. His family had been unable to join him until much later. He never got to watch his children grow up.

With those last words, a wave of sadness came over him. 'But,' he added, 'I was lucky enough to be able to open up my own shop, and since I married young, all three of my sons are already at university.'

All this man had needed to reclaim his pride and dignity was for Farhad to show him some interest and kindness.

Back home, Farhad spent the rest of the evening reading the memoirs. He reached a section that detailed life in Isfahan in the tenth and eleventh centuries. He found himself fantasising about that splendid civilisation where everyone, regardless of origin, lived together in mutual respect and understanding. Islam was liberal in those days. Muslims considered Abraham, Moses and Jesus to be prophets, and believed that God was present in the universe, in dialogue with his creation. Yet this inclusive side to Islam was being increasingly eclipsed.

The day of the auction came on that Monday morning. Once he was back from his run, Farhad put on jeans, a white shirt and a blazer and headed over to Sotheby's to inspect the sale room. He consulted the catalogue and worked out that lot 188 would probably be put up for sale

at around three o'clock. He had time to go out, get some
lunch and have a look around Mayfair.

At half past two, he returned relaxed and easily found a
seat near the front. People trickled in and soon the room
was full. He had never been to an auction before and was
struck by the electric atmosphere among the bidders, in
strong contrast to the typically British, nonchalant attitude of the auctioneers. As bidding began, more and more
hands started to shoot up. Each lot was taking longer to
sell. His came up at around a quarter to four. After a series
of three mediocre Qadjar paintings, the stone was put up
for sale. It seemed rather nondescript in its plastic box.
Farhad was surprised to hear a murmur pass through the
room. His heart started pounding in his chest. Others
were obviously aware of this piece which he had only
found out about the month before.

The stone started at its base estimate. It soon went up
to his bid. That did not surprise Farhad as he waited for
the sound of the hammer to confirm it had been sold
to him. His heart dropped when he heard the bidding
start up again. An unremarkable man on his left had just
smoothly placed a bid without batting an eyelid. Soon the
offers were flooding in, and he was outdone by one, then
another. A fierce battle ensued and the stone was sold for
the absurd price of £7,500. Farhad's neighbour, who had
already introduced himself as an English dealer, leaned
over. 'They say the stone has special powers and that it
once belonged to the founder of a medieval Iranian sect.
My client wanted it at any price.'

Farhad did not respond, too absorbed in keeping his eyes fixed on the buyer as he left the room. The bidder had not needed to show his number, so he must have been well-known. An intrigued Farhad tried to catch up with him but didn't manage to clear a path through the crowd in time. Instead he doubled back and asked an assistant auctioneer if he knew the name of the client who had bought lot 188, claiming that he wanted to contact him with a counterbid.

'He's a middle-man who usually buys for Mr Al-Morabi, a wealthy businessman from the Gulf, who lives in Abu Dhabi. You haven't got a chance against him,' he added, his eyes glued to the main screen where bids were rapidly mounting for the next lot. 'If I were you, I would leave it be. I've already had several counterbids.'

Disappointed that he had not managed to acquire his stone, Farhad went straight home. He turned on his computer and began searching the name of the purchaser. He tried various possible spellings, but to no avail. On the off chance that Sergeant McGuire might know something, he sent an email to Scotland Yard. He instantly got a reply, asking him to come by straight away.

Farhad gathered that this must be an important name, since Scotland Yard avoided ordinary means of communication.

'His name is on our list,' the sergeant announced as soon as he saw Farhad. 'He comes to London every now and then, and he's one of the visitors we take a keen interest in. We haven't yet figured out what his game is, but you're on to something. He is a powerful man. He may turn out to be a major benefactor of home-grown terrorism, but then again, he might not. It wouldn't be the first time. In any case, you're making progress. In the last ten days you have already managed to uncover the names of two big fish. Just you wait, it won't be long before we're offering you a job,' he added with a twinkle in his eye.

Farhad had never imagined that there could be a link between his two strands of inquiry. With this revelation, he started to think that there were people who wanted to construct an ideological link, even if one didn't really exist, either to capture people's imagination and legitimise mass indoctrination, or to promote a past, more enlightened Islam. Either way, with the stone they had identified a key object with great symbolic power.

He felt bereft, deprived of an artefact that had belonged to his ancestors. He had done everything in his power to get the stone back, but he felt as though he had failed a mission that had been passed down the Safandar family for ten centuries. He burned with anger when he thought of the man who had stolen it from them.

Now the stone had been sold, Farhad was tempted to return to Paris. But he was held back by the feeling that he hadn't yet given the report his all. He didn't want to disappoint his sponsors.

He rallied when he recalled a quote from Churchill that his great-aunt used to recite to him: 'Success is the ability to go from failure to failure without losing your enthusiasm.' So far, there had been no failures. Reza had not yet chosen a side. The stone was just a minor setback. He remembered he had a train to catch for Oxford the next day. Karim had so spontaneously invited him. Reason told him not to do anything rash.

He wouldn't leave London just yet.

That evening, the memoirs captivated him more than ever. He had reached a chapter about his family origins, and he was thrilled to have found such a treasure trove of information. Real-life knights seemed to jump out of the yellowed pages. How incredibly evocative writing could be! His ancestor described the Javanmardi Knighthood, whose code of chivalry was set out in Ferdowsi's *Shah-nameh*. Their quest was of a spiritual order. They sought the truth and strove for attributes such as generosity, nobility of soul and a moral compass. Knights had to set high standards for themselves, stopping at no less than perfection. Nader the Elder described with pride how they had also inspired others, such as the military monastic Order of the Templars. These two knighthoods had shared a mutual fascination with each other, even if they had principally been adversaries.

Farhad was enthralled by the accounts of alliances formed between the Assassins and the Templars or the Frankish crusaders to combat the Sunni Arabs. His interest was captured by this idea of an 'alliance of convenience'. He slowly realised that the tales of the memoirs, these exemplars of spiritual, mystical chivalry, were where the real treasure lay. What mattered was living according to your values. In comparison, the stone, fascinating though it may have been, was nothing more than superstition. Just like his ancestors, Farhad would refuse to be taken in by legends of its supposed magical powers. He did, however, remain curious to read Hassan Sabbah's engraving on the stone. He vowed to locate the three fragments, now scattered across the world, and to reunite them so that he could be enlightened. That evening, something told him that he would succeed.

X

It was early afternoon and the air was crisp when Farhad made his way to Paddington. He was aware of British scholars' high standing in Islamic studies, and he knew how much respect they had for Persian civilisation. He was keen to hear what they had to say. The train journey was an hour long, and Worcester College about a ten-minute walk from the station.

Although there was something slightly austere about Oxford, it was a welcome change from London consumerism. He felt as though he were on familiar territory, as the architecture reminded him of Yale and the Ivy League institutions. He had to acknowledge, however, that American universities were only pale imitations; this was the real thing.

The colleges were scattered among townhouses, little shops and many booksellers. Farhad watched as young people quietly walked or cycled past. Each college name engraved above the pediment brought to mind the authors and philosophers who had studied there, from Erasmus, Hobbes and Keynes to John le Carré. As he walked past, he caught glimpses of the imposing cloister-style quads through the narrow doorways. Every now and again, snippets of electric guitar or booming speakers would blast out from the half-open windows, just as from any student dorms. On the way, he dropped off his bags at the Randolph Hotel, not far from his meeting place.

As he stepped into Worcester College for the first time, Farhad was struck by the juxtaposition of its monastic architecture against the liberal attitude of the students. 'A true Abbey of Thelema,' he mused, recalling Rabelais's ideal campus.

Footsteps rang out through the quad. Karim was coming to get him at exactly half past four. He smiled at Farhad and led him to the Senior Common Room, reserved for post-graduate students and young tutors in training.

'Would you like a cup of tea or coffee?' Karim asked as he plugged in a slightly battered old electric kettle. 'We've got a bit of time before the lecture starts. Actually, it will be more of a debate; the professors will only speak for ten minutes each.'

Karim was clearly in his element. He was a very likeable young man, full of life. Farhad noticed a group of students sitting in one corner of the room. Their exuberance seemed incongruous with the formality of the setting. They chatted for quite some time and Farhad felt himself relax.

The tone of the lecture was established from the outset, and the energy in the room was palpable. One of the professors, dressed in a black gown, stood up. He took to the podium and outlined some of the branches of contemporary Islam, by way of introduction. Some sects were founded on dogmatism, inspired by archaic, warmongering precepts and a hegemonic mindset. This approach had made waves in Muslim countries. Iran, the first country to go down this road, was already backtracking, but a series of increasingly virulent followers in other countries wanted to follow in its footsteps. He cited fundamentalist groups in Indonesia, Thailand, Saudi Arabia and Egypt.

'Political Islam may lead to a new form of totalitarianism,' concluded the professor. He gave the floor to a colleague who nuanced the discussion.

According to the next speaker, several branches of Islam had coexisted throughout history. However, some had sought to take centre stage. Nowadays the most dominant factions in our societies were those affiliated with Wahhabism, and to an ideological doctrine established by the Muslim Brotherhood in the 1920s.

Farhad and Karim looked at each other, pleased to see they were getting to the crux of the matter. The professor went one step further by bringing up the Nahda, a reform movement also known as 'Cultural Renaissance' or 'Enlightenment', which had swept right across the Arab world by the beginning of the nineteenth century. Through dialogue with the West, certain intellectuals had authored critical readings that called into question the conventional interpretation of the Quran. Others even proposed contextual readings of the texts, but the ensuing controversy had forced these pioneering minds to flee their countries.

'Moreover, dear colleagues,' the professor concluded, 'the West offered them no assistance. Pushed out to the margins of our societies, the defenders of reform could not go on. This was a grave error, which would prove costly to the West. As, indeed, it would to all the moderate Muslims who would have supported progress, but instead are now subject to serious pressure, whether they remained in their home countries or have emigrated to ours. Intimidation aimed at silencing progressive voices.' At these words, a wave of hands shot up from the audience.

'Have there not always been extracts of the Quran inciting violence?' asked a woman in academic dress. 'What do you make of the verses that the terrorists draw on?'

'Thank you for bringing up that important point,' the speaker responded. 'Many theologians agree that the inflammatory verses in the Holy Book can be traced to the time when the Prophet Mohammed was under threat, and when this new religion was using military means to spread its influence across the Arab world. Today, these verses are redundant, except for those who seek to advance militant Islam.'

'Which just goes to show how essential it is to read in the context of our time,' added the woman, her arms outstretched.

'We certainly hope that some of the parties concerned will begin to work in that direction.'

The third speaker took to the lectern to address the

situation in those London boroughs and Northern cities with large Muslim communities.

'Undereducated, underprivileged communities are pressurised by their imams to change their lifestyle. Those who don't comply are accused of being bad Muslims, even traitors. In some cases, their code of honour overrides the law of the land, which is clearly not sustainable.'

This last speaker was Albert Ridley, a world authority on the topic, and Farhad listened to him intently. At the end of the panel discussion, Farhad found himself sitting at the High Table of Worcester College's great dining hall. According to an old Oxford tradition that had become English etiquette, politics, religion and work were not to be discussed over dinner. So instead the guests discussed the Holbein retrospective in the new wing of the National Gallery. They also talked about the perceptive BBC programme which had recreated his famous double portrait *The Ambassadors* and adapted it to the modern era: a prime example of contextualisation.

Farhad was only half listening, more interested in the animated students who were roaring with laughter on the long tables below. At the end of the meal, they retired to a private sitting room to enjoy a hundred-year-old cognac and Farhad finally had a chance to approach Professor Ridley. He congratulated the don on his speech, as they had a shared belief in the need to promote a more nuanced and plural vision of Islam.

The professor fixed his keen eyes on Farhad. He argued that though they were sorely needed, there were very few

Muslims who dared to question their religion. Nonetheless, it was a battle that had to be fought, as too many Muslims were suffering in silence or were gradually being won over by radical, fundamentalist ideas.

Determined to prevent the spread of such views, Farhad put forward a plan to organise meetings that would propose alternative readings of the Quran, based on examples drawn from everyday life. The aim would be to illustrate that as early as the seventh century, the Quran had comprised two distinct parts: the surahs of Mecca, dictated to the Prophet by the Angel Gabriel, which concerned liturgy and monotheism; and the more political component written in Medina, which corresponded to the time when a threatened Mohammed declared Holy War.

The old professor was impressed by Farhad's intellect and wished to continue this discussion of one of the greatest problems of his time. They arranged to meet in college the very next morning.

'You must be one charismatic guy to have caught his attention,' Karim exclaimed. 'And he wants to see you again tomorrow! Did you know he's considered one of the toughest tutors in Oxford?'

Farhad was deep in thought. This evening had been eye-opening. He was grateful to Karim for inviting him along.

Alone in his hotel room, he picked up the phone and dialled his mother's number. She was not in, so he left a short message in a reassuring voice. Then he called Bardia and told him all about the last few weeks, taking care not to dwell on the episode in the mosque so as not to worry him. He interrupted his monologue to check if Bardia was listening.

'I'm all ears,' Bardia replied. 'I've even switched the TV off – you're making me miss the football! I'm more interested in your battles.'

They spent a good hour on the phone, drawing up Farhad's plans. Talking it through helped him put his thoughts in order. At the end of the call, he described the evening he had just spent in Oxford.

'You have to go for it, even if it means staying in London for a few months,' Bardia urged. 'What could possibly be more important than helping to make the world a better place? Remember the here and now,' he added, quoting the famous *hic et nunc* that they had adopted as their own personal catchphrase ever since secondary school, when they learned it in Latin class together.

Farhad had always wanted to do good. For the first time, he had a real shot at it. Bardia then asked after Reza, and Farhad answered without going into detail. His friend promised to come and see both of them soon.

By the time he woke the next morning, the last few doubts had evaporated from Farhad's mind. He had a meeting at Worcester College.

At nine o'clock, he knocked on the professor's door.

This morning, in his cosy rooms with books stacked

high in the many nooks and crannies, and his dinner jacket swapped for tweed, Professor Ridley looked nowhere near as imposing. But one thing hadn't changed from the night before, and that was the inquisitive spark that still glistened behind his glasses. Though the conversation had stayed fairly light the previous evening, Farhad was soon to grasp the level expected by academics here, in Britain's top university. Ridley's questions came at a steady pace, one after the other. The professor had watertight backing for every counter argument, and it took all Farhad's conviction and mental agility to stand his ground.

'So, young man,' asked the professor, 'how do you plan to change the behaviour of people here? Their allegiance to the imams is unwavering, as you may know. Every fatwah is practically a divine edict.'

This fired Farhad up, 'Not all Muslims are extremists. Those living in the West practise a moderate religion, if any at all. Some don't associate themselves with any religion. Most of them have never opened the Quran. Now, we should be encouraging them to read it, so that they can form their own, independent opinions rather than letting themselves be manipulated through ignorance.'

The professor nodded. Farhad had captured his attention. 'Communitarianism has wreaked havoc in Britain and Holland, especially for the younger generation,' Ridley argued. 'Inward-looking communities are moving towards a more radical Islam. Is that something you were aware of?'

'Yes, I am working on a report for an American institute

and I have observed that drift. There are universal values in the Quran which the radicals don't even mention. They want to suppress any reference to the experts who have put forward alternative interpretations.'

'More often than not, those who attempt alternative readings of the Holy Book are hampered by the religious leaders themselves,' objected the professor. 'The famous Egyptian Al-Azhar University, which has boasted of its mission to safeguard and defend Islam for over a thousand years, is in fact responsible for standing in the way of alternative readings. Some of the works by thinkers questioning the overly doctrinal side of Islam are inaccessible.'

Farhad, too, was sceptical of what Al-Azhar stood for, but he disliked hearing it criticised by a foreigner.

'Was that not the very same Egyptian university which saved Aristotle's writings from being destroyed? And was it not Averroes who, by writing commentaries to those texts, contributed to their circulation throughout Europe, thus saving the works of several Greek philosophers? The School of Toledo translated Arab texts, including those of Avicenna, from as early as the twelfth century. Bridges have always existed between East and West. The important thing is to keep them open, and to build on them. Of course, we are living in a time of severe obscurantism, which discourages independent thought and reasoning, but that hasn't always been the case. For instance, in Spain in the eleventh century, an intellectual advancement encouraged a real dialogue between Muslim scholars and their Greek, Jewish, Persian and Christian counterparts.'

Ridley seemed deep in thought. At Oxford, great importance was given to convictions and to the way you defended them. The professor had been testing the young researcher's determination, and he was satisfied with what he had heard.

'Those theologians' texts drew heavily on Greek culture and have been adopted into Islamic thought,' Farhad continued. 'I should remind you, if I may, that the first time Avicenna's writings were banned, it was by the Catholic Church at the Paris Council in 1210. Although the ban was dropped in 1231, it goes to show that the Catholic religion has serious limitations of its own. Was it not that very same church which burned irreplaceable books for over five centuries? I am sure the Muslim world will come to a realisation, too. Our job is to help them reach this point, and that task is easier than people think.'

The professor's gaze was fixed on Farhad from behind his glasses. He had glimpsed in his accurate analysis a real hope of seeing a new generation determined to take the issues into their own hands. He interrupted and asked one final question, with British pragmatism cutting through Farhad's passionate language.

'The development of radical Islam is clear to see,' the professor said. 'We are in complete agreement on that point. But what do you intend to do about it? Writing reports is no longer enough.'

Farhad took his time before he responded. Having seen the intense pressure and indoctrination that people were being subjected to, he had thought of setting up discussion groups to counter these influences. Ridley approved of his plan. That was indeed a very good idea. Unfortunately, they had run out of time. The professor had another meeting with a student very shortly.

'If I may, I have one piece of advice for you,' said the professor as he got up to say goodbye. 'You should spend some more time in the UK. It's an excellent setting for the sort of work you are interested in. I suggest you call the Director of the University of London's School of Oriental and African Studies, on my recommendation. They are currently looking for a replacement for the upcoming academic year. You could be a visiting fellow. The position would allow you to meet students and professors of some standing who are working in similar fields. I'm sure you would be of great help to them. But whatever you end up doing, try to remain as independent as possible. Otherwise, you will make yourself an easy target for fundamentalist criticism. You will be seen as aiding and abetting the British, no matter how valuable your work may be,' he concluded, with a kind expression on his face.

Farhad left enheartened. A weight had lifted off him.

XI

The train for London had pulled away from the Thames Valley and was running alongside a forest where the leaves were turning an autumnal brown. Farhad was absorbed in his notes from the panel discussion. As they passed a cricket field, he looked up and out of the window. Young Pakistanis and Hindus were playing alongside their English school mates. They were all wearing white; their school sports kit, no doubt. Through their shared education, they would have the chance to grow up free, not shackled by racial prejudice.

The next morning, the chancellor of the University of London, Mr Tahsen, gave him a warm welcome. Just a week before the start of the academic year, one of his professors had informed him that he was going on sabbatical. This young Iranian, referred by one of the leading experts in Islamic studies, was a godsend.

'Let's cut to the chase,' he declared, getting to his feet. 'You come highly recommended.'

He began by outlining the kind of course he was looking

for: a series of twenty-five lectures on the philosophy of religion, with a strong focus on Islam abroad. Farhad was delighted. He did, however, insist on hermeneutics, the history of interpretations.

Mr Tahsen agreed to take him on for a trial period. He offered Farhad a salary high enough to cover a comfortable living in London, one of the most expensive cities in Europe. It was decided that, as assistant professor, Farhad would be able to structure his own course around the topic they had set out. Mr Tahsen wanted to see him again as soon as possible, as he would have to slot the classes into the timetable.

The following Monday, Farhad moved into a one-bedroom flat in Montague Place, not far from the university. Its two large French windows led out into a tiny garden, with a little table and wooden chairs where he could work. Just the other side of the low wall was a communal garden, shaded by two elms and a large blue cedar.

Content with the flat's space and high ceilings, he opened his suitcase and began to unpack. He arranged his few books on the shelves, and then went to get dinner. Out of the numerous restaurants, the local Indian was the only place that served food so early. He had a quick vegetable *biryani* and went back outside, keen to explore the lively streets. People were so different in this country! Life in this sprawling metropolis, just as anywhere, had its difficulties and challenges, but they were not in the least bit confrontational.

He spent a restless first night in that house stirring at

every little sound from the street. He did not feel at all ready for his first class even though he had spent the best part of the previous week preparing for it. Sleep finally came at dawn

He woke up at nine o'clock, his room bathed with light. Karim was due to come over soon so they could work together. He got dressed and went out to get a coffee. A little Italian café caught his fancy. There was a mixture of students and office workers in dark pinstripes, some of them crowding around the counter.

'*Un espresso, per favore,*' he asked.

An Indian waiter served him, and Farhad drank up. Karim was due in less than ten minutes.

Back home, he jumped when he heard the piercing bell echoing off the empty walls for the first time. As Karim came in, he was beaming. The pair sat down to work and immediately differed over the outline of his seminars.

Karim felt it was important to show students the range of knowledge they would acquire through attending his classes. He also suggested that Farhad dedicate one lecture to Islam's other cultural influences, particularly the other two major monotheistic religions. Farhad was beginning to see his point.

At around noon, they went out for a bite to eat. There were less than four hours to go until the class. Farhad took Karim to the little Italian café. It was quiet, so they could get on with the lecture plans in peace.

Thanks to Karim and his passion for public speaking, Farhad's first lecture went down very well. He was relatively unperturbed by the mass of faces all looking expectantly his way. He got straight into the topic with all the enthusiasm of a great lecturer. He skilfully handled the religious concepts of Islam, Judaism and Christianity, showing how they had adapted to the changes in European history over the centuries. He demonstrated the major influence of Christian and Jewish advisors over Muslim princes in Spanish Al-Andalus, who had allowed Spain to live peacefully alongside other European monarchies for seven centuries. He cited examples of pious Muslims who were integrated into and held in esteem by societies where Catholicism dominated. Often dervishes were the wisest figures in eighteenth-century anti-clerical literature, such as Voltaire's works. Anecdotes came to Farhad as he was talking. He described how Persian gardens had inspired replicas in every European court, how the dishes of many feasts had been influenced by the East; and how their turquoise, encrusted amber and other precious stones had been collected by royals.

At the end of the class, he barely had time to catch his breath before, to his surprise, he was surrounded by students all commenting on his lecture. Some were about his own age. Among them was Karim, who passed on their compliments and reported back on his enthusiastic reception.

'It was fascinating. You had us all glued to our seats! And you seemed completely at ease.'

'New ideas kept crossing my mind as I was speaking. I really enjoyed teaching.'

Farhad spent the remainder of the afternoon planning his upcoming lectures. Karim was right. In order to raise awareness, he had to move away from chronological order and instead focus on describing good people in tolerant, open-minded societies.

He would dedicate several weeks to the Moorish period in Spain. He had so much to say about the philosophers and scientists who, through their translations of the great texts, had been the first to build bridges between East and West.

He wanted to spend plenty of time on the Sufis. Had they contributed to a fruitful exchange between East and West?

Week after week, Farhad noticed an increase in attendance at his lectures. A majority of his students were from the Middle East; young Sunni or Shia Muslims, whose parents and grandparents had emigrated to Britain during decolonisation. One day, while he was making reference to the Holy Book, he quoted a surah and turned to ask them a direct question.

'I assume you have all read the Quran?'

Some seemed to tense up. Others avoided his gaze. Farhad asked again. He gathered from their unanimous response that most of them had not. They seemed to fear that reading it would push them into extremism.

'Did you know that the first part of the Quran has incorporated the principle of forgiveness, so central to the Judeo-Christian tradition? If out of curiosity you read the text, especially the first section which corresponds to the Mecca period, you will find the verse: "*In the name of God most merciful to those who are themselves merciful*" at the beginning of almost every surah.'

But since the students seemed not to be on the same page as him, Farhad went back to the main theme of his lecture to recapture their attention.

At the end of the lecture, a young woman came up to him. She was attending his lectures as an unregistered student. Her questions, as unusual as they were pertinent, revealed an insightful mind. She had a particular charm, and spoke animatedly. Her brown eyes studied him intently as she pointed out that the verses on forgiveness underlined above the surahs had been added in the tenth century. Farhad maintained that mercy was integral to the Quran; it could be seen in the fifth surah, for instance. She frowned, seemingly unconvinced. As he did not have the text in front of him, he proposed to organise meetings outside class, to read and talk about certain passages of the Holy Book.

The students around her approved, but she seemed a little disconcerted. Then, her eyes brightened as she admitted to Farhad, 'Everything I know about the Quran I've learned at university. My parents would be worried if they knew I were reading it. They distance themselves from anything to do with Islam.'

'I can understand that,' he told her. 'I was in a very similar situation back home. Where are you from?'

'My family is from Uzbekistan, but I was born here. *Kheili khoshbart shodam...*'

She spoke to him in Farsi, having guessed he was Iranian. He smiled at her, pleased to hear his own language spoken so well with an accent he would have been unable to identify.

'That's the only thing I can say in your language,' she added hastily, afraid he would strike up a conversation. 'I'll come along to your discussion groups – they sound interesting.'

Farhad suggested they meet at his place as Bloomsbury was so close to the university. He was delighted to have an excuse to read and debate the Quran.

The meetings began the following Sunday. Farhad tidied the flat and arranged his chairs in a circle for a more informal atmosphere.

Neila was the first to turn up. She did not have far to come since she lived on campus, she said. Noticing that the walls were bare, she offered to lend him some Persian miniatures picked up at Bermondsey flea market. They were of no use to her while she was living in student accommodation. Farhad gladly accepted. She finished arranging the cushions in his sitting room with him, agreeing that a circle would help to break down the teacher-student hierarchy. Karim arrived shortly afterwards, laden down with the takeaway he had decided to order from a Lebanese delicatessen. Neila helped him put the falafel, kibbeh, hummus and pita bread out onto trays. When Farhad tried to pay him back, Karim turned down the offer, explaining that this way, he wouldn't have to catch the last train from Paddington on an empty stomach.

A few timorous students came in. When there were enough to begin, Farhad poured the tea as he explained how he proposed to proceed. He hoped no one would be offended if the Quran were studied from a historical or anthropological perspective. He wanted to adopt a simple reading in order to try to understand it. Discussions among students would be most welcome. But in no way was he suggesting they would question its contents.

This arrangement was well received. The first meeting confirmed Farhad's hopes: the students were keen to take a different approach to Islam. He aimed at guiding them to understand the scope of the Text and its present relevance. The students' level and enthusiasm promised to make for an in-depth discussion.

At the end of the evening, he recommended the students read *The Tolerant Quran,* a short book written by Dalil Boubakeur, imam of the Paris Mosque. He also suggested they get hold of a paperback copy of the Quran so they could highlight excerpts which could be read as a code of conduct compatible with Western civilisation. They then shared the delicious meal Karim had brought.

The gatherings went on regularly at Montague Place, with newcomers each session. The debates became increasingly animated. Farhad wanted his students to analyse their religion from a philosophical standpoint. At the end of one meeting, Farhad asked them to consider a sermon given by Soheib Bencheikh, an imam from Marseille.

'When the prophet says, *Teach your children riding,*

swimming and archery, today that should be translated as
Teach them English, IT and the internet.'

The question of the adaptation of the Quran's message
to the modern day was a difficult one to address and
Farhad expected it to provoke a very polemical debate.
But to his great surprise, the discussion the following
week was fruitful and constructive.

Soon, there was too big a group for Farhad's little
one-bed flat. The meetings attracted many students in
search of a sense of identity. As the autumn was mild,
the circle spilled over into the garden under the watch-
ful eye of Mrs Holland, the landlady who lived on the
second floor and was intrigued by the sight of so many
dark heads down below. She liked young people and had
kept in touch with the university. She met all of the students who were interested in or writing dissertations on
Oscar Wilde, her husband's grandfather.

During these sessions, Farhad was learning alongside
his students. He was keen to understand the very essence
of the Quran, whether on a spiritual level or otherwise.
His great asset was his ability to remain neutral. He listened to discussions without losing his cool. His main
priority remained encouraging his pupils to accept other
points of view, as he had set out in the second meeting. All
differences were welcomed and deserved to be debated;
attacks against specific religious groups would not be tolerated. He was aware that tensions were rising between
Sunnis and Shiites. One, the Shiites, recognised Mohammad's descendants and his son-in-law Ali as the spiritual

heir. The Sunnis, on the other hand, had instated Abu Bakr, a trusted friend and confident of the Prophet, as first caliph. But he was focused on teaching his students to see past their differences.

When they were getting to know each other, Farhad and Karim had debated the distinction between the two branches of Islam, the former being Shiite and the latter Sunni. But they had soon come to the conclusion that if Muslims could not get on between themselves in their host country, how could they ever hope to live in harmony with Jews and Christians?

'What unites us is stronger than what divides us,' Farhad was fond of repeating.

XII

No matter how intense Farhad's life had become, Reza's silence continued to weigh on him, and his friend was never far from his thoughts.

He had found out through Bardia that Reza had a girlfriend. Bardia had run into him in Portobello as he was buying a little lace blouse. They had exchanged a few words, a bit of banter and a hug, before going their separate ways. As he watched him walk away, he had noticed a dark-haired young woman take his arm.

Later, Reza had told him that her name was Samia and that she was the sister of Nabil, who had got him his job at the foundation.

Farhad nodded. He worried about his friend and was keen to arrange a meet-up again soon.

Attendance to the Islam discussion group continued to grow. Once the weather turned cold, the garden was no longer an option, so Farhad was forced to ask the director of the university if he could book a room. Given the popularity of his lectures, Mr Tahsen was well disposed to him, and assigned him an auditorium in a nearby more outspoken in the discussions. One evening, the basis of Farhad's beliefs was attacked for the first time by a young student.

Farhad stood up to speak. 'I'm a believer but I believe in an open-minded Islam,' he answered. 'We are here to understand all facets of the Quran. The other two religions, of which Islam is the continuation, have always been in favour of interpreting their Holy Books. The Word of God is not crystallised in a single text. Indeed, they say it exceeds and goes beyond the Word. Averroes, the great scholar, used to say that you can philosophise and search for truth while still believing in His Word. Does Allah forbid us from educating ourselves, or from making use of our capacity for interpretation? Believing and trying to understand are not mutually exclusive. Why would God have endowed us with reason if He had not intended us to use it?'

At this point, Parvez spoke up, 'I am a practising Muslim. But in our family, we prefer to pray in the privacy of our own house or in the back of our shop, while we seek to integrate in public. Today, fundamentalists demand that Islam determines every aspect of our lives. But I disagree. The very reason I was forced to leave Pakistan, my native land, was because sharia laws were being brought in and it was becoming intolerable.'

Another student asked Farhad, 'Professor, what do you make of the surahs which advocate crimes against the infidels? How do we reconcile this with integration?'

Farhad hesitated. Like most of his fellow believers, he

was greatly perplexed by these incitements to violence, but he hadn't yet dared to address this critical issue.

Parvez took advantage of Farhad's silence to speak out.

'These incitements do exist, as many of us are aware. But they shouldn't shape our reading. Radical Islamists interpret the word *qatala* to mean "killing" whereas it should be translated as "fighting". The greatest jihad is the fight against oneself, as we are told by surah IX, verse 5. Or self-defence, as set out by surah II, verse 194. War is presented as a last resort. In the words of the Prophet, "it must be treated with contempt". It would be a real mistake to be put off the whole Quran merely on the basis of those misunderstood surahs. These new believers are dragging our most vulnerable children into a war against the West. This is not the message of the Quran. You can be a good Muslim without wanting Islam to become the dominant religion in the world; that idea has been much contested by many great commentators of the Quran. We have to focus on other Islamic precepts.'

'We don't doubt your good intentions,' responded the same student, 'but by sugar-coating the Quran, you are playing into the hands of the extremists.'

Parvez lost his temper. 'It's by refusing to engage with the Holy Book that we play into their hands! You can't reject everything in the Quran because of these surahs. They have to be read in context. They correspond to the time when Islam was expanding, when the threatened Prophet had to leave Mecca for Medina in 622. Our primary duty is to combat ignorance. Remember, Islam did not win over our homelands through violence. Syria, Egypt, Persia, North Africa, Libya and many other countries became Muslim not through war, but because those who did not convert had to pay an additional tax.'

Farhad was stirred by these wise words.

'This was our tenth meeting,' he announced at the end of the session. 'We have explored some new ideas, and I urge you to reflect on them. Above all, we must not be ashamed of our religion, even though some use it to commit horrendous acts. That is a perversion of Islam for political ends, a form of fascism. We must go back to the texts, get to know them and pass that on to our children and future generations, shedding light on other aspects of the Holy Book. That is how we can protect the most impressionable from manipulation.'

The time had come to grasp the nettle.

One Saturday as Neila was passing Montague Place, she rang Farhad's doorbell and waited, in the hope that he would be at home. He popped his head out of his ground-floor window and smiled at her. He had just come in from a run, and invited her into the living room, suggesting that she helped herself to a cup of the excellent Darjeeling tea he knew she'd like. A few minutes later, freshly showered, he brought in a tray with a few oriental sweets.

'The last meeting was pretty intense – you didn't look too comfortable,' he said as he was coming in and out of the kitchen. 'Why don't you join in and voice your opinions?'

Neila tried to explain. She had listened to students as they laid out their reasons for mistrusting Islam. She was aware of the religion's contradictions and multiple interpretations, so she had no hard feelings towards those who critiqued it during the discussion groups. She had heard the very same arguments throughout her child-hood. However, she felt that the tone had hardened, and this concerned her. She had brought one of her broth-ers along to one meeting, a fairly introverted boy who was nonetheless interested in what they had to say on the Quran, but their discussions had irritated him. He felt they were not achieving anything concrete and he had argued that the theoretical approach wasn't getting anywhere.

Since then, she had chosen to prioritise work on the ground, as generations of Muslims were completely disil-lusioned. Most of them were on the poverty line without any hope of improving their situation. Society had to give them a chance and offer them reasonable opportunities for the future. And as there was no time to waste, she had decided to get involved with communities directly. There, at least, she could get things done. They had to engage with Northern cities where poverty was skilfully exploited by the fundamentalist movements.

Farhad listened, rapt.

She began to describe her work outside the university, and the conclusions she had come to after several months. She was alarmed by the behaviour of some imams in the North who were exploiting impressionable Pakistani communities.

'But in their homes, people are not so easily swayed,' he objected strongly. 'It is up to each of them to exert their free will. When I was in Bradford, I noticed that the people there were very worldly. Most of them…'

She interrupted him, surprised and reproachful that she should have to pull the wool from over his eyes.

'You don't get it, Farhad! Parents listen politely when the imam pays them a visit, glad to get it out of the way, and then they go back to their business. But young people are more vulnerable and lack a sense of purpose, so they let themselves be won over. Home hasn't taught them the first thing about Islam. They dive in without asking questions, they force their sisters to wear the veil and beat them up if they see them with English boys. Last year, a girl was burned alive in one of the suburbs.'

Her honey-coloured eyes lit up as she spoke. The chink of winter sun shining through the window formed a halo above her wavy hair. Farhad's mind began to wander. Neila was his brightest student, she was the one who had given him the idea for his discussion groups. He was grateful to her and felt comfortable around her.

'You're in your final year now. What would you like to do after university?' he asked.

'I've decided to spend a few years doing humanitarian work in the towns where the Islamist pockets are most virulent. As of next month, I'm planning on renting a one-bedroom flat in Bradford so I can be right at the heart of the work and get more involved in the community.'

Farhad felt a twinge of regret. She wouldn't live just up

the road anymore. These last few months, he had been so busy that he had hardly given her a second glance despite the fact that she was his neighbour. But he could see her clearly now, her uncompromising courage and stunning beauty. He remembered that the only pleasant afternoon he had spent in the last three months had been with her, wandering around Camden Market. Neila had become part of his life in London, and he didn't want to lose her. He moved towards her and gently put his hand on her arm. She looked up in surprise. She had never thought anything of visiting him alone. His eyes stirred something inside her, but she pretended not to notice and turned her mind back to the problems affecting the communities.

'She's so much in her intellect,' he thought as his fingers moved slowly down her arm. Her skin was soft and velvety, like the tender leaf of a lime tree in early spring. His hand met hers and he clasped it. She stopped talking, both surprised and amused by this unexpected move.

Farhad avoided her gaze; he didn't want to dampen his mounting desire. He took time to take in her body through her clothes, guessing her shape under her sweater, her narrow waist, and tracing her contours with just his eyes. Her hips were barely visible, covered modestly by her jeans, and yet he longed to lose himself in them. He hesitated for a moment. A student and a teacher. A young Usbek and an Iranian. Overcome by his emotions, he swept away such geographical and social considerations. He knelt down, took Neila's face between his hands and kissed her slowly. Her lips were as soft as peaches and parted under his. Still kissing her, he loosened his embrace and paused so she could move away if she wanted. She undid her shirt with the same determination she showed in life, curious to experience new sensations, and safe in the arms of a man she believed to be genuine and sincere. She gave into pleasure, free in her body. Farhad was greatly moved by the serene young woman who gave clear reign to her desires and was carried away by his.

Being together multiplied their strength, each wanting to keep up with the other.

Neila did not go to Bradford. She chose to set up her organisation in Southall, a suburban area near Heathrow airport. Entire Pakistani families had moved from Punjab fifty years earlier to work in a tyre factory, and they had settled there. They had been joined by Sikhs, and, more recently, by Afghans.

Neila started a women's group and a tuition centre for young children to help improve their grades, and to which she dedicated nearly half of her time. She also worked with young girls who refused to wear the veil and women who wanted to find jobs in order to free themselves from marital constraints. Some of the stories she heard made her blood run cold, so blatant were the injustices.

Within a few months she could see the part played by some institutions in the drift towards Islamic fundamentalism that had begun in Britain in recent years. Charitable organisations were opening free schools for children from underprivileged families, with their curriculum going unchecked. Neila was spending an excessive amount of time in Southall at the expense of her studies. As she was guaranteed to get her bachelor's degree at the end of the year, she was mostly focused on her association and was even planning on expanding her work to other towns.

Farhad could not help worrying about her and was relieved when Neila told him two women had offered to help. One was a plump and cheerful mother of three; her happiness was infectious and the young girls warmed to her instantly. The other younger woman was less outgoing and found it harder to assert her authority. Neila promised herself she would introduce them both to Farhad.

Little by little, Neila started bringing women to the Tuesday lectures. For most of them it was their first time in a university. More and more were asking to come along.

Parvez and his wife, both still very concerned about their eldest son's departure, floated the idea of setting up monitoring task forces in different communities, in order to identify those likely to fall under influence. As they had no news of their eldest, they blamed themselves for not acting in time, and they wanted to start a project to help other parents.

Farhad liked the idea. He also saw it as a good way to enlist his most committed supporters and put to use the skills that they had acquired in their native land, but which were not necessarily recognised in Britain.

Family monitoring centres were set up in order to protect the most vulnerable young people.

He and Neila helped Parvez to create public-run task

forces in difficult areas, which would bring together those wanting to get involved. A small, motivated group of men and women from these quarters would meet to combat the downward spiral into radicalisation. It was vital to counteract the mistrust that had gradually developed between the British communities and their own. Racism was beginning to rear its head in the land of tolerance, particularly in the North where many Muslims were living in almost total poverty.

Parvez, who was building a reputation for himself in their circles, gradually began to bring together discreetly a few reliable people from all sectors who would carry out internal investigations and keep an eye on the young people at risk. Their argument was irrefutable: terrorist attacks could only exacerbate existing tensions, even within the peaceful and moderate population, since they would pitch groups against each other. Muslims themselves would be the first to suffer the consequences of the violent actions of a few indoctrinated kamikazes and there was already a rise in racially motivated crimes. Farhad and Parvez were adamant to protect the life of their community as well as that of future generations.

After a few months, Farhad's Tuesday sessions started to make headway. For some parents, they were a source of renewed validation for their identity, providing a deeper historical and philosophical perspective. They gave them the words to speak with their children. Many were convinced that outsiders would not be able to protect their youngsters from the pull of radicalisation, and that they themselves had to open a path to a non-violent Islam in line with other religions. That was the mission they had to accomplish. Any other interference would serve only to heighten tensions. Thanks to their work, young people would be better armed to respond to the growing number of subversive preachers in their local areas.

Though their qualifications may not have been officially recognised in Britain, they brought their skills together. Engineers like Parvez were called on for technical and organisational questions. Intellectuals and teachers were encouraged to speak out in their communities and to advise young people on their future. This mission would make it easier for them to accept a lack of development in their careers, where they were confined to lesser positions. Farhad insisted on one important point: if anything suspicious were uncovered, he wished it to be kept from the police and dealt with internally, so as to retain the trust of as many people as possible and avoid any accusation of being informers. Mistrust towards Scotland Yard was deep rooted.

Sometimes after their meetings, Farhad suggested to those still hanging around in the lecture room on Tuesday evenings that they continue their discussion in a small Afghan restaurant not far from Bloomsbury. All would converge still enthused by the ideas they had shared.

In the almost empty restaurant, the night would slowly transform. Neila would take an *oud* hanging from a nail on the wall near the counter and it would start vibrating beneath her fingers. The soothing melodies would transport the listeners to Central Asia, to lands where they had never been. In the candlelight, her eyes seemed to gaze into the distance, and her voice rang out, melodious and low; a voice from another era. Farhad was each time deeply moved by her natural gift. Neila had been taught traditional songs by her grandmother, and she had inherited her vocal skills.

The music was infectious. Like arabesques pushing back the walls of a labyrinth, the quarter tone phrasing captured their imagination, so accustomed to Western culture, and their minds, so strained by long days of studying. London and its hubs faded into the background. Rationalism and Enlightenment dwindled to pale flickers that would have to be rekindled in the morning. As the music filled the air, their thoughts escaped to lands they had not ventured to for many years. In their mind's eye, each of them would glimpse a faraway land, and snippets of a childhood where *djinns* used to hide in the gardens and sleep under the Persian carpets. Every so often, one of them would share these thoughts out loud. And then they would all be of one mind, invited to share his past, journeying into their lost paradise together.

Karim would get caught up in the atmosphere, quoting verses from the great Sufi poet Rumi, or Sophocles. He jumped from one to the other, fusing them in a spatial and temporal melting pot as he saw fit, at ease with this productive mingling of East and West. For every text, and every word, he adopted a tone so perfect that the others fell silent. Those were evenings of blessed fulfilment and wholeness.

Then, late at night, the little group would walk back to the Montague Place flat. A bed would be made up for Karim on the sofa. Farhad and Neila withdrew to their bedroom, lovers until sunrise.

XIII

One morning, Farhad received an email from the director of the Yale Institute congratulating him on his report.
He had particularly appreciated Farhad's contributions to
a spiritual and enlightened Islam that all Muslims could
identify with. Adopting the non-linear reading, as Farhad
recommended in his conclusion, was not just advisable,
but essential. He agreed that the extracts inciting violence
could be traced to a historical era when Islam was under
threat. He backed this up with a citation from surah III,
verse 7: 'As for those whose hearts are devious, they stick
to the most obscure part of the Quran, seeking dispute
and discord.' He also reiterated that it was vital to adopt
interpretations which would contribute to the common
good.

Bolstered by his approval, Farhad dared, for the first
time, to name his endeavour. With their work, he and his
group had come to symbolise a new kind of Westernised
Muslim who offered a middle way in the interpretation of
the Texts. They would set themselves entirely apart from
current preaching while respecting traditional Islam. In

his workshops, he would strive to shine a spotlight on and reconnect with classical Islam. In order to do so, he would showcase great figures whose exemplary life epitomised Enlightened Islam, such as Saladin, a Sunnite sultan from the twelfth century, who was universally recognised for his magnanimity when he conquered Jerusalem against the Crusaders.

By bringing these individuals back to life, Farhad hoped to demonstrate that they had no need of extremism to thrive.

The following day, Farhad received a letter from the American ambassador to Great Britain. The office of the director of Yale had invited him to a reception, where he would meet the US Secretary of State, who would be in London in April in preparation for the G8 summit.

After careful consideration, he turned this offer down. What good would it do to meet politicians? With Ridley's advice in mind, he feared he would only lose the independence and neutrality he had always prided himself on. His report was now behind him, although he was pleased that it had been read by influential figures.

Furthermore, the day of the reception clashed with the opening night of Karim's play in Oxford, and he would not have missed it for the world.

Farhad had found Karim to be an excellent work mate, who provided invaluable help for his lectures. A real friendship sparked up between them. 'Two heads, one mind,' as Karim had once put it.

The rather argumentative, young Sunnite researcher challenged Farhad's convictions, backing him into a corner to prepare him for his classes. To motivate him, he would remind his friend of the cruelty of perfidious Albion colonialists. His anti-colonialism was even more marked than Reza's, and although Farhad mostly agreed, he took great pleasure in teasing him about it.

Karim's true passion was theatre, but as a very reserved person, he rarely discussed his preferences. Farhad and Neila knew he was rehearsing Shakespeare's *The Tempest* with a theatre group from his college and were adamant they would go along and support him. As he didn't open up easily, they knew very little about him besides the fact that he was particularly gifted and advanced: he had almost completed his PhD.

Yet despite his capabilities, he rarely dared to voice his opinions in the workshops. This frustrated Farhad who wished he would get more involved, but at the same time was loath to push him into anything. He was thrilled when Karim came up to him one day after a lecture and announced, 'I had always planned on becoming a teacher, but after meeting you, I realise that there are more urgent things to be done. How about if I came to work alongside you for a few months once I get my doctorate, to see how it goes?'

Farhad thanked him, choked up with emotion. Karim was the first to offer to help, and in accepting to devote his time he was paying his endeavour a great compliment. With Karim at his side, he would be so much stronger.

Still he thought he should point out some of the more tedious sides of their work. And he tested the waters by warning him that the most urgent task was to secure funding.

'We can't expand our work without substantial financing, given the powerful opponents we are facing that use charities and promote free education in Koranic schools. If we got endowed with sponsorships, we'd also be able to set up an independent office and pay our full-time employees. Volunteers can only be a back-up.'

'I should be able to help find sufficient funding, especially since I won't need a salary to live in London, at least not to start with.'

Farhad looked up, unable to conceal his surprise. Karim was on a scholarship and lived a normal student lifestyle. Farhad had never brought up his background, since it didn't matter to him.

'I inherited some money from my maternal grandfather, so I didn't think I'd need to ask my father for anything. But the more I get involved, the more I think we could ask him to help our cause.'

Karim had been too uncomfortable to reveal his parentage. His father was an important emir, but up until then he had not seen any point in mentioning it. Having been brought up as a prince, he had struggled to adapt to the Scottish school where he had been sent at the age of six to toughen up. He had been teased so much about his background that he had papered over his heritage. He dreaded going back to his native land to pick up the torch.

Seeing the relief on his friend's face at his measured response, Farhad realised just how keen he was to escape his fate for a few more years. History was offering him the opportunity to reconcile his two aspirations: to help the Muslim cause and to continue studying the texts. Such a clear vision for his future would provide the motivation he needed to call on his father.

A few days later, Karim announced that he was going to spend a week with his father in Dubai.

XIV

Persian New Year had come around again. Every Iranian home was getting a thorough spring-clean in preparation for the Norouz celebrations.

The festival, which coincided with the spring equinox, still had the power to bring together Iranians spread across all four corners of the world. Ever since Zoroastrianism had become Persia's official religion, families would lay their table with *haft sin,* seven elements symbolising rebirth which all began with an 's', the letter 'sin' of the Persian alphabet.

Farhad had been invited to share the celebrations at some friends of his mother, so he set aside his troubles for the evening and got ready to observe this beautiful tradition. He put on a dark grey suit which he had not worn since his dinner at Oxford, along with a navy blue overcoat, and set off for Knightsbridge. He came out of the Underground in front of Harrods and walked along the shop frontage towards the sparkling boutiques of Sloane Street.

He was very worked up, having just spent the afternoon

in Brick Lane where a large part of the Victorian Spital-
fields market had been replaced by Norman Foster's swish
new offices. To his dismay, some of the Bengali community were still living in sordid squats nearby, probably
soon to be evicted. On the other hand, while visiting their
mosque he was pleasantly surprised to discover that it was
a listed place of worship; built as a Protestant church, a
plaque in Hebrew indicated that it had also been used as a
synagogue for a hundred years. He was thrilled to see this.
He also appreciated the Latin inscription below a sundial
on the façade: UMBRA SUMUS. It was a phrase that
some of the Londoners from wealthier boroughs would
do well to remember.

London had developed a luxurious, consumer lifestyle. According to some, over the last fifteen years it had
become Europe's new Babylon, despite the economic
crisis of which effects were starting to be felt. In the chic
parts of town, fat cats dressed in black, or in glitz and
glamour, would roll up to pricy restaurants in Rolls-
Royces and sports cars. Most of them were foreigners;
Russian couples whose wealth remained a mystery; young
Europeans who had come to study in the land of Shakespeare; or the growing number of intelligentsia from Gulf
royal families who were coming in increasing numbers to
escape the restrictive Koranic law and oppressive climate
for a few months each year.

The younger generation lived in London all year round.
They met in the cafés on Beauchamp Place and Crom-
well Road. Certain streets in Knightsbridge, with women

in hijabs or full-face veils, could almost have been mistaken for more Eastern cities, whether it was day or night, summer or winter.

The cultivated Englishmen, whose subtlety and euphemisms had made a name for their country and created the universal myth of the gentleman, were nowhere to be seen. They must have been turning in their grave to see such a change, consoling themselves with the hope that this era would not last. Would globalisation continue to transform every Western capital into a modern Babylon that the wealthy would continue to seek out? More and more, as the gap in wealth and revenues grew larger, violent reactions would be inevitable. What did it say about the city that a major hospital in Hyde Park Corner had been converted into a luxury hotel, where London's affluent flocked to lavish charity dinners at £10,000 per table without anyone batting an eyelid?

It was not yet dusk when Farhad arrived at Cadogan Place, still mulling all this over. Petals of Japanese cherry trees carpeted the large garden lawn and the pavement underfoot. Lost in his thoughts, he didn't notice them, nor indeed the taxi drawing up beside him in the side street.

A smiling woman greeted him in Farsi, '*Salam*, Farhad, *kheili khoshhal shodam.*'

'Mina!' he exclaimed. 'What are you doing here? I thought you were in San Francisco?'

She gestured to him to wait a minute while she paid her fare. He nodded, delighted to hear his own language. Her familiar voice had transported him back to his homeland.

'I didn't know you would be in London!' he said, kissing her warmly on the cheek.

'Neither did I,' she chuckled. 'It was a last-minute decision.'

'How long are you staying for?'

'I am here for Norouz and I go back to California at the end of the week.'

Together they walked up the white stucco steps and into a large living room where they were welcomed with open arms. This clan reunion was starting to put Farhad at ease; he went to talk to an amiable man who had called him by his first name. He could not place his face. After a while it came back to him; he was a good friend of his father's who had also moved to London. Farhad finally relaxed, wondering how he could have spent so many months away from his nearest and dearest, apparently without missing them. Neglecting to do so had unknowingly weighed down on him,

The doorbell kept ringing. More and more guests arrived in a slight haze of cigarette smoke. Then, as Farhad turned his head instinctively towards the door, his grip suddenly tightened around his glass. Reza had just walked in. He moved smoothly, seeming to glide from one guest to the next. All heads were turned towards him, waiting to say hello. He spent a few seconds with each, adapting his conversation to be light or serious depending on who he was addressing. 'He is always effortless,' Farhad thought, observing him from his vantage point by the doorway. He had selected a pastel green tie, in accordance with Norouz tradition, to complement his midnight blue suit. Yet, as Reza came closer, Farhad was the only one who noticed a certain unease on his face; a completely different expression he'd never seen before. His smile was forced. He seemed to be struggling to look people straight in the eye. His gaze demonstrated not his interest in the people he was talking to, but his inner turmoil. It seemed as if another man had taken over Reza's soul.

'He's obviously concerned. Perhaps it has finally got through to him,' thought Farhad, and his heart wrenched.

At that moment, he hesitated. Should he avoid him, or confront him? The decision was made for him; Reza was coming towards him with a wide smile on his face.

'I'm so happy to see you!'

'Are you? Forgive me if I'm a bit sceptical. I'm not too keen on fickle friends,' Farhad replied.

'I thought you had gone back to France,' protested Reza, sensing his friend's anger.

'It wouldn't have been hard to find out either way,' Farhad snapped.

They were interrupted by other people coming over to greet them. This interlude allowed Farhad to get a hold of himself. Once again, he became very cutting. When the guests asked what had brought Reza to London, to everyone's surprise, Farhad answered for him, 'He rubs shoulders with people working in some dubious charity sponsored by certain Saudi Arabian families.'

Before he could go on with his sarcastic jibes, their

hostess called them to the dining room where a custom-ary magnificent buffet was laid out. With whetted appe-tites, the guests dived into mountains of pistachio rice flavoured with orange peel, duck with pomegranates, veal with aubergine, and fish on a bed of *sabzi polo*. All these traditional New Year dishes should have lifted Farhad's spirits. Yet, while he was waiting his turn, as Reza shot him a fleeting glance, his nervousness was palpable. He had his tell-tale, barely perceptible frown, which since they were children had been a sign that he was aggravated.

As they headed over to the buffet, Reza tried to defuse the situation by light-heartedly asking Farhad what he was up to in London. But Farhad did not seem keen to talk about himself. He gave Reza a look of disdain, mut-tering that he was a coward and a pawn in the game of international terrorism.

Reza shrugged and left the queue. He would rather walk away, as there was no way he would let their disa-greement be a blight on their families' honour. This was polite Persian society; a sanctuary on neutral ground.

Forgetting all sense of propriety, Farhad left his half-filled plate on a table and followed him into the drawing room.

'How are those friends of yours from the foundation?'

'Now's not the time or place,' Reza replied coldly. 'But since you're interested, I am developing a plan which I'm sure will surprise you.'

This ambiguous statement merely exasperated Farhad even more. Reza took him by the arm and led him to a corner of the room. Farhad followed willingly. The guests were drifting back to the living room, their plates full.

In a low voice, Reza explained how, after their meeting, he had made some enquiries himself, starting with verifying the organisation's accounts. Charity work was only one part of the Al-Rhubni Foundation's work. Their other activities were, indeed, highly subversive. He spoke freely, relieved to have a friend to open up to.

'I just hope they haven't picked up on me,' he added fearfully. 'I'll tell you more tomorrow.'

Farhad, who had listened silently, was troubled by that last remark. He offered to have him discreetly put under Scotland Yard protection, but Reza took offence and refused outright.

They had to stop talking as their hostess, pretending not to have noticed their discomposure, was asking: 'Aren't you eating anything?'

She led them back over to the buffet, her mind set on feeding those poor young men who were so often deprived of good Persian food. She had cooked everything herself and they were going to enjoy it. The tension between the two friends had not slipped her notice. She took care to keep them apart, discreetly asking her daughter to stay with Reza while she looked after Farhad. She got him to sit on a sofa next to her and asked after his mother, his cousins and his great-aunt so persistently that the friends did not get to exchange another word for the rest of the evening.

Farhad hardly slept a wink that night.

Was it pride or criminal intent that had stopped Reza from giving him news for all those months? And if they had not met that evening, how would he have found anything out? Had mixing with those shady characters taught Reza to lie? How could he have complete confidence in him when he had made so little effort to get in touch?

Farhad went back over all of Reza's facial expressions from the evening. When speaking to him, he had seemed authentic and sincere. So why did he get the feeling that Reza wasn't telling the truth? Where did that mistrust come from? Had he chosen to bring him into the loop merely because he had realised how much he already knew?

If Reza thought he was in danger, why was he refusing to be protected by Scotland Yard? Did that mean he was on the terrorists' side?

Unless he was simply faithful to his principles? After all, didn't Farhad in his own workshops consistently use the argument that Muslims should avoid outside help?

He didn't feel any further forward when he woke up the following morning with a muddled head. He grabbed his phone to see if Reza had left him a message. Nothing. But it was still only eight o'clock. He went to the mirror to shave. The night had been haunted by his worries, which had drawn dark rings around his sunken eyes. He had to pull himself together. A lecture hall full of students would be waiting for him in less than two hours. He reread his notes and left for the university.

Neila noticed that he was exhausted. She thought that the evening's excursion back into his own world had left him wistful. If it had crossed her mind that he might have met a woman at the New Year's dinner, she would have been very hurt, but she didn't dream of it. She knew her partner worked in his own way, and there was no point in prying. Nonetheless, she had never seen him like that before, so she stayed behind after the class.

Farhad seemed lost in thought. He smiled when he saw her and they exchanged a few affectionate words. She had back-to-back lectures all afternoon, so he decided to go home, and they agreed to meet for dinner. On his way out, Farhad turned on his phone. His heart jumped. A message from Reza flashed up on the screen. He wanted to meet the next day. Farhad hesitated. This encounter could be decisive for their friendship. He could well lose his dearest friend. Yet he saw no other way to convince him of his good intentions.

He was glad to get away from campus so he could think things through. He had never mentioned Reza to his new friends. For the first time, he felt isolated, out of step with the rest of them. Why did Reza want to see him now, after leaving him in the dark for months? Was it just because they had met at dinner, or had he meant to get in contact with him as he had suggested? He was bitter that his friend had kept his distance for so many weeks, leaving him sick with worry. He had lost precious time while an attack was potentially being planned against the people of London.

Reza had suggested a discreet meeting place, on the banks of the Thames next to an abandoned wharf in the Docklands.

Farhad came out of the tube, almost bumping into a group of executives in pinstripe suits standing in front of their bank on the corner of Threadneedle Street. He had decided to walk the rest of the way to put his thoughts in order. He could not afford to make the slightest criticism or show any hint of emotion. There was too much at stake.

He spent the rest of the journey thinking back over the best moments of their childhood. Reza was the brother he had never had. He was a few months his junior, but Farhad often let him take centre stage so as not to scare him away. He had always been afraid of losing him. The inseparable pair had learned to compromise early on in the summer months in the gardens of Ramsar.

A touching detail came back to him. As small children, when their two families had dinner together, they would slip away at the end of the meal, leaving the adults with the sweets and fruits. One time, they had ventured up onto the flat roof of the house and Reza had pointed out the shifting constellations. They had spent hours marvelling at the heavens and their perpetual movement. That evening, they designated that roof as their hiding space to be used if anything bad happened. It was their little secret. Their impregnable fortress. Nothing and nobody could reach them there.

Farhad also enjoyed spending time there alone. Once

when he was perched up there, he had heard his aunts looking all over for him. The doctor had arrived to vaccinate them. His cousins had already lined up for the injection, but he was nowhere to be seen. Reza had been roped in as they were sure he would know where to find him. Reza had searched with the family without giving his friend away, despite his fear of Farhad's father.

He also remembered the time in Tehran when, after an earthquake, both families had slept side by side on mattresses in the garden. It had been such fun for them both, two young boys oblivious of danger.

When he arrived at the bridge at a quarter to six, Farhad could still feel the warm wind blowing through his hair and the delicate scent of that night. He had his anger under control. He had been moved by the memory of Reza as a child, but his sharp mind was prepared for the revelations which his friend was about to share. What conclusions had Reza come to? His mind had certainly changed.

He caught sight of Reza striding through the haze. He stiffened slightly when they embraced. Farhad looked straight into his eyes. He did not wish to appear too emotional even though he found it hard to conceal his feelings. He resented the fact that he had left him to suffer in silence. Farhad had prudently decided not to tell his friend about the recent developments in his life in London, and intended to stick to it. This made the encounter somewhat contrived.

Reza's story was long and detailed. Farhad listened to him impartially. He made a huge effort to control himself and to appear detached. The wind had started to blow and the murky water was choppy, but neither of them noticed.

Reza explained that once he had got over his anger, he had decided to investigate the heart of the organisation himself. He had used his role as treasurer to request an audit and had had a copy of all the accounts of the international branches sent to him. He had come across some bills which kept reappearing on a regular basis. Maroush, a Lebanese caterer, was delivering a meal for some twenty people on every second Wednesday of the month to an unknown address connected with their organisation. And there was another clue. Charities based in Kashmir and the north of Pakistan had received very large sums, though no major disaster had taken place there recently. The earthquake in Kashmir was long ago and their donations had been assigned to the four previous yearly accounts. Reza concluded that the organisation was funding other unknown activities.

His suspicions had been further aroused by a memo that instructed him to settle the bill of a certain Zyad, Director of the Al-Tarabi Institute of Mathematics in Pakistan. His name had cropped up again because he was expecting a large sum to be sent to a foreign account and had asked why there had been a delay in the transfer. Reza had checked: there was no centre, school or university in Pakistan with that name. He had dug deeper and found a ticket from British Airways that had been made out in the same name. This man was due to arrive in six weeks.

Something big was in the offing, but he didn't know who to talk to or what to do.

As he was speaking, Reza's darting eyes revealed how worked up he was. Clearly he had intended to deal with this alone, but he was now asking for help. Farhad kept his cool, as he recalled Reza's long silence. The story was all plausible, but he found it hard to trust him completely. Yet his friend never lied. He had always been discouraged from lying by the strong emphasis their education placed on loyalty.

He waited for Reza to ask him about his work in London. He wasn't forthcoming. If the directors of the foundation had got wind of his activities, they might well have sent Reza to infiltrate them.

He figured that, if Reza had not been recruited as a double agent, he was putting his neck on the line by contacting him. What he had done was a great testimony to their friendship, and it moved him profoundly. Now, he had to restrain his pride.

Farhad had learned a lot in the last seven months. Reza seemed very fragile to him, and he took him under his wing. He needed to be given the strength to fight on. Taking care to regulate his breathing and avoid showing any emotion, Farhad described his investigation, the pressures Muslims were subjected to in certain English towns, and the honour code that could lead to the murder of young women who refused to comply. He told the story of Jezabel, burned alive by her own brother because she wanted to marry an Englishman.

Farhad could tell that Reza was becoming infuriated.

'We mustn't succumb to this intimidation. If there is a lesson to be learned from all we have endured over the last ten years,' said Reza, 'it is that everyone must be allowed to choose if and how they practise their religion. We have to fight the infatuation with ill-adapted Koranic laws and show the British that our faith is compatible with Western culture. But I agree with you, for now we have to focus our energy on doing everything in our power to stop the terrorist attack which will also affect generations of Muslims. I have one request: we must avoid involving the authorities.'

Farhad agreed. 'While good relations with them are desirable, vital even, working too closely with the police could be interpreted as betrayal.'

Together they decided on a plan of action. Faced with the dangers Reza had revealed, they decided to communicate only by short handwritten notes in a set hiding place. For their meetings, Reza suggested the greenhouse which was always open in the Chelsea Physic Garden. They arranged to meet there the following day.

The wind was getting stronger and buffeting the waves in front of them, so the two friends had to cut their talk short.

On his way back towards Bloomsbury, Farhad was still trying to come to terms with some of Reza's contradictions by going over parts of their conversation in his mind. What he had said corresponded to some elements of his own enquiries about the charitable foundation. He had to believe his account, even if there was only one chance in ten that this plan was real.

There was far too much at stake.

XV

Farhad was calm and composed when he arrived near the Physic Garden late the next morning. As he walked alongside a white wall, he went past a very art deco Italian restaurant where a waiter was finishing off polishing glasses. He thought of taking Neila there for her birthday. She seemed quite worried since the Norouz dinner where he had been unable to bring her. He had not told her about Reza. He did not know how to describe his friend, given the doubts that were plaguing him. She had opened up to him describing his guardedness as a lack of trust. He had been apologetic. This slightly rough patch had confirmed his true feelings for her. Farhad had realised that he was very much in love.

That morning in Chelsea, this thought filled him with a peculiar happiness. With Neila by his side, he could move mountains.

He walked across Swan Walk, noticing the trailing wisteria as he went by the long brick wall. There would be no way of telling that there was a delightful garden hidden behind. He went through a barely visible little door and was greeted by hundred-year-old olive trees towering over an assortment of medicinal plants, geraniums and Persian lilac bushes. The low hum of the traffic and riverboats on the Thames in the distance was the only reminder that this was in fact an urban garden. He went down the central path past the borders of lawns. He spotted the grey wooden bench, tinged yellow with lichen, and sat down to wait for Reza, glad to be early. In such timeless surroundings, he felt a little meditative. This was, as he had just discovered, the oldest botanical garden in England after that of Oxford. He caught glimpses of greyish hair bustling about behind the green hues of foliage in front of him. A woman was leaning down over the lilac irises and the feather palms.

This garden was full of surprises. Its unlikely combinations of plants conjured up an image of colonial England, when slightly eccentric people would dedicate their lives to identifying and collecting rare species.

He heard footsteps crunching on the gravel and saw a breathless Reza pass in front of the shelves of flowers without even noticing them. He sat down a short distance away and then got up after a few minutes, once he was sure he had not been followed. All these precautions would have seemed ridiculous had Farhad not noticed that his brow was furrowed with anxiety. They met in the greenhouse.

Although the windows in the roof were half open, the heat was stifling. All of the fern species were packed together in this tight space. Some had grown to an unbelievable size. Reza agreed to resume the conversation from the previous night. For their hiding place, they picked a large, flat, mossy stone to the right of the pond, which was covered in tiny water lily leaves. They would slip their documents underneath the stone and would avoid being seen together again until all was over. They exchanged a meaningful look as if to seal their agreement. Then, in order to cut short any sentimentality, Reza took a couple of steps over to the door at the end of the greenhouse and opened it with the ease of someone who knew the place well.

The two friends, united in their resolve, hurried down the half-wooded path out into the sun. They jumped when they heard a crackling noise to their left. The grey-haired lady had just tossed some branches into her battered wheelbarrow and had already started up again.

Farhad felt his heart swell at the sight of that frail figure, evocative of the nineteenth-century English ladies who went off to every corner of the world in search of rare plants. An Alexandra David-Néel of roses and irises. In and of themselves, those women epitomised a tolerant civilisation with a global outlook. He admired them. He felt his resolve harden. He would not allow fundamentalists to change minds, instil hatred and racism, and create irrevocable divisions at the heart of this nation.

They walked past a long narrow pond reminiscent of those in the earliest Persian gardens. They reflected on them. Reza, who was starting to relax, told Farhad that he had become an active member of the Royal Horticultural

Society. This meant that, on weekends, he could visit gardens which were closed to the public, where he could clear his head. Their peaceful conversation was suddenly interrupted by a splash. A duck had dived into the pond to escape the unwanted attentions of two drakes. The noise brought them crashing back to reality. They went their separate ways, leaving behind that enchanted, timeless symbol of an England, an oasis from vengeance and fanaticism. They had agreed that each time a new document was put under the stone; they would let each other know through a mobile number used only for that purpose. Every day, they would take care to change the SIM cards that Farhad had bought especially.

As a final precaution, nothing personal would ever be mentioned in the text messages. They would only use the sentence 'The flowers have arrived' to indicate that a letter had been dropped off in the greenhouse. The only exception would be in case of an emergency.

This method worked very effectively for some weeks. Reza's reports were short and to the point. Farhad would read them and immediately draw up a list of questions which he would leave under the stone. Reza would go to pick them up and give detailed answers in his next report.

In one of his messages, Reza shared some vital information; the plot was taking shape.

There was to be a meeting in New Haven, a minor Channel port, at half past six on the 7th of May. A group of five men with British passports would be waiting in a white Fiat Ducato. A sixth man would take the wheel to pick up the brains behind the operation, arriving from Pakistan. He had a code name but Reza thought it had to be Zyad, since the dates on his plane ticket all matched up.

The most urgent question was the identities of the conspirators. Who were they? Farhad wanted to know their names at any cost. Reza replied that there was little hope that he could get his hands on the list, and certainly not anytime soon. However, against all odds, two days later he triumphantly left a very optimistic-sounding message on his friend's voicemail.

Farhad rushed over to the greenhouse.

Of the group of collaborators, Reza had got his hands on three names, dates of birth, addresses and occupations. Two of them were from Birmingham, and one from Southall. They were paid regularly by the foundation, but seemed to have no active role. They must have just been recruited for the '7th of May mission'.

They finally had something concrete to work with. Now they could draw up a plan and put together a strategy. There was no other solution but to take the places of the three men. Farhad then asked for some more details on the attack, adding a short 'well done' in the margin of the message. In his hurry, it did not occur to him to explain to Reza how he intended to take down these criminals.

Nor was Reza aware that Farhad already had the means, as well as a tight-knit group of highly motivated men. They didn't take much convincing. Once he had put them in the picture, he gave each of them a specific task to carry out.

Parvez would be in charge of the two men from Birmingham. He had good contacts there and would have no difficulty in getting in touch with them.

Neila was brought up to date that same evening. Given the gravity of the situation, she could at last understand her partner's secrecy. She would be responsible for the man from Southall. She had to act fast and find a way to approach him. She decided to close her organisation down during the Easter holidays to give herself the time she needed.

XVI

Despite the imminent danger, spring light shimmered over the great island of Albion. As he took his brisk morning walk, Farhad wondered if the Greek god who had lent her his name would protect Britain against adversity. He noticed the leaves uncurling with the sudden rise in sap and his resolve strengthened. Nature always had the great gift of refocusing him. He could now feel the life force deep inside him on full alert. He was determined to prevent a crime from being committed in the name of a distorted interpretation of his religion. Whatever the risk, he would see this through.

He was pleased with how eagerly Neila and Parvez had accepted their tasks.

The next evening, Neila came back with news about the man from Southall. He was a socially withdrawn bachelor. He worked in a tyre garage and he only kept in contact with his sister, a married woman with two children. It would not be difficult for Neila to offer them free extra-curricular support.

The two young boys did indeed need a hand with structuring their work, so their mother jumped at the opportunity. Neila was struck by how intelligent they were and took great pleasure in going to their house three times a week to teach them spelling and maths.

She described to Farhad how they would wait for her by the door, with neatly combed hair, holding their workbooks. She suddenly seemed so involved with them that Farhad did not dare ask when she would get down to the matter in hand.

One afternoon, the grateful mother asked her to stay for tea. Neila accepted and took the opportunity to enquire whether she had some family in Britain.

Her brother was very fond of his nephews and often came over to play with them. Nevertheless, she sometimes worried about his influence on them. The children's favourite uncle was twenty-eight and had been addicted to poker for some years. Their indignant father had disowned him, which had pushed him even further into an almost irreversible isolation. But his sister believed that he was a hard worker with his heart in the right place. She had found him the job in the garage where he was a diligent employee, but she did wonder if he made enough money to pay his debts. Just recently he had seemed to stop worrying. Someone had offered him help, apparently with no strings attached. He had been an easy target. The money had boosted him, and he now appeared to be in better shape.

Each time they met, Neila reported back to Farhad on the progress she was making. She was stunned to see how impatient he was for results; he was even harsh at times. She didn't take it personally, putting it down to stress. After all, D-Day was approaching.

At last she managed to meet the brother and could sow doubts about the good intentions of his 'benefactor'. He refused to believe her at first, but she warned him that he would soon be called upon to fulfil his side of the bargain.

'I'm sorry, but there's no mistake,' she told him. 'You and your loved ones are in grave danger.'

It was only when she mentioned the fateful date that his eyes opened wide and he began to listen. For the sake of his sister and her children, he agreed to let someone take his place.

Parvez used his connections to contact the two men in Birmingham as Farhad had asked.

The first was a waiter in a very popular Halal restaurant. The eldest child whose family had stayed behind in Pakistan, he had settled in Birmingham with great ambitions to learn a trade. After a few months of struggling with precariousness, he had decided to postpone his dream. Living in a basement in a very poor area allowed him to save up and send most of his wages to his brothers and sisters, as he believed was his duty. What little remained was hardly enough to pay his rent, but since he was fed by his boss, he got by. One of the regular customers, whom he held in great esteem, had mentioned a foundation which helped Muslims in exile, and had offered to pass on his application.

After several weeks, this friendly man came back, smoothing his elegant moustache as he told him that his application had been accepted.

A sum equivalent to his salary would be transferred to his account each month, the only proviso being that he swears an oath of allegiance to his religion. The young man was over the moon, and already had visions of his brothers joining him in England, of paying for their education, and of how proud his mother would be. Not once had he wondered why he was being given such a sum.

When he met Parvez, a well-respected figure in the London Pakistani community, he had no qualms about telling him his life story, and in so doing he revealed some useful information. The customer was called Nabil. It didn't take much for the waiter to admit that he was ready to help out his benefactor on the given date. The Pakistani grocer needed all his skill and paternal sense to convince this good-hearted man of his benefactor's dishonest intentions.

'You have unwittingly been recruited by a terrorist group masquerading as a foundation. I don't know how else to put it.'

The young man went from surprise to despair; then despair to disbelief. He called Parvez a dirty liar, making him question his approach. The grocer feared that he had failed. Then, after a moment of silence, he thought he should mention how his son had also been recruited.

'I'm part of an organisation whose aim is to protect young, well-meaning people such as yourself. These terrorists take advantage of your good nature to commit atrocious acts. It is absolutely vital that you agree for someone to take your place at the rendezvous in order to avert an attack. Many lives, including your own, are at stake. Logistical and financial aid will be available to help you out. We will always be at your side. We are trained for this; it's our job. You have nothing to fear,' he added as he was leaving.

Before returning to London, Parvez alerted his local contacts. The Easter holidays were coming to an end, and the last person they had to persuade, a young student who lived on campus, would soon be back at university.

While he waited for news, the grocer spent the next few days serving his customers in the shop, much to the dismay of Farhad who could not understand how he could work so calmly when such a horrific plot was being hatched.

Parvez bided his time, waiting in vain for a call. Eventually he decided to travel back to Birmingham, and he was on the train when his phone rang. The boy was back.

His informant was waiting for him at the station. He had managed to obtain an identity photograph and some of the young man's personal details. He was traditional-looking, with a warm, smiling face. He was rather slender, often wore a tweed jacket and spent most of his time in the library with his head buried in theology books. His only hobby was in the evenings, when he and his friends would go bowling together. That would be the easiest place to spark up a conversation.

Parvez made up his mind to go to the alley that very evening. Screams of delight and frustration, clashes of rolling balls and crashing pins bounced off the walls. He took a step back in bewilderment. How would he be able to find him in that horde of people? He decided to take a look around the room anyway. He stopped to watch a player who was about to bowl. His face was straining with the effort. His dark eyes focusing on his target, he threw the ball and it trundled down the right side of the lane. He sharply flicked back the lock of hair that had got in his way at the crucial moment. He had only managed to knock two pins down, so he walked back to collect his second ball, past the spot where Parvez had stopped. All these young people looked as though they had stepped out of a Bollywood film. Even if he did locate his target, he would never get the chance to approach him here.

Some rather pretty girls cheered when, on his second attempt, the remaining pins wobbled and were knocked down. The player clenched his fist, revealing his competitive nature. A friend came up to congratulate him and then apologised sincerely as he bumped into Parvez. The latter turned around to assure him it was nothing, only to find the tweed jacket right in front of his eyes.

Here was his chance to strike up a conversation.

Realising that Parvez was Pakistani, the young man took pleasure in revealing that he was from Tajikistan and they exchanged a few words in Tadjik.

Parvez asked him about his studies. Under the pretext

that his son was studying the same subject, they arranged to meet the next day.

They bonded when Parvez brought up the philosopher Dariush Shayegan, and the student was enthusiastic about his theory supporting religious plurality. Parvez was relieved. This young man was far from being an extremist.

It was easy to convince him not to carry out a task that might cost him his life.

XVII

The progress made by Parvez and Neila was not enough to allay Farhad's fears. He went over and over the situation in his mind. They were caught at the centre of a terrorist plot, dealing with attackers who would stop at nothing. But he was still missing so much vital information. In response to Reza's message, he couldn't resist bombarding him with questions about the attack itself. Two days later, he was notified that a new message had been dropped off. As soon as he got a chance, he headed to the Physic Garden.

Quieted by the familiar noise of the gravel crunching beneath his feet, he barely noticed that the dahlias were in full bloom as he strode into the greenhouse. The air was slightly less stifling this time as it was early in the morning. He went straight to the stone to retrieve the message. Reza's report was to the point and written in his characteristically neat, if slightly rushed, handwriting. The three men had accepted their mission. The attack would take place near a square in the centre of London. They did not yet know how the operation would unfold, but he had learned that they had already done a trial run. Farhad knelt down to lean against a flat stone and compose a short reply. He pressed Reza for more information about the meeting in the van.

Days went by with no news from Reza. Farhad was irritated. They didn't have long. Conscious that time was ticking on, he dropped off another message, emphatically urging Reza to respond.

He was, however, aware that his tone might not be to Reza's liking. Especially since he had been so caught up in his own work, he had omitted to tell Reza about the team he had behind him.

Reza may not have asked any questions, but this did not mean he wasn't thinking intensely. Didn't Farhad have any idea of the danger he was putting himself in each time he dug a little deeper? Had he no appreciation of what he was going through? How on earth was Farhad planning on foiling an intricate plot in a foreign city that he hardly knew? Besides, all this haste and pragmatism was very unlike Farhad and it didn't seem unreasonable for Reza to conclude that this behaviour meant he was acting under orders. Had he gone back on his promise not to speak to the British authorities? What if he were working as an informer for MI5?

As worried as he was, Farhad hadn't seen Karim since his return. But they had spoken and he knew the emir had agreed to support their cause. They had arranged to discuss it further on the opening night of *The Tempest*.

Although Farhad had been looking forward to spending that evening in Oxford with Neila, on the day he felt sick with worry.

Obsessing over the imminent danger facing Londoners, he kept changing his phone's SIM card.

Still no news.

How could he leave while Reza might be in danger? He contacted Parvez, whom he hoped would find a way to infiltrate the affiliated branch of the foundation. He urged him to act fast.

Parvez didn't ask redundant questions. He reported for duty at the association that same day.

He acted the part of a newly arrived immigrant searching for a job. He was politely greeted by a woman dressed in a smart suit and a light muslin headscarf. She suggested he look through the job offers on file in their mini-library. There was an opening on the premises for a floor cleaner, and he put in an application. The woman looked him up and down, and told him he could start immediately.

Once she had shown him around and equipped him with brooms and dusters, the former engineer got to work. This was a godsend. He could stay on the premises and wander the corridors as he pleased, without arousing suspicion. His son would fill in for him at the grocery shop.

He was instructed to start with the toilets. He willingly complied, almost glad to be assigned a task that would bring him closer to his target.

It wasn't easy to find Reza. He went from room to

room without passing many people. Behind a glass door, a young man with thick dark hair caught his eye, but he could only see his back. He seemed quiet and focused. The plaque on the right read 'Treasurer'; Parvez's hunch had been right. He was hanging around, polishing the glass, when Reza stood up, sensing that he was being watched. He was tall and stylish in a grey suit with no tie. It all matched Farhad's description and Parvez left to tell him the good news.

When he learned that Reza was 'quiet and focused' in his office, Farhad flew off the handle. Parvez thought he was overreacting, so attempted to calm him down by describing the atmosphere in the office.

'Don't forget that it's April. The books are being closed, so he is probably very busy,' he concluded.

Farhad snapped out of it and was composed enough to ask Parvez to stay at the foundation for as long as possible. They needed to know more. He told him he shouldn't hesitate to call any time he had news, and reminded him to keep an eye out for texts.

On the train to Oxford, Neila did her best to be cheerful, but Farhad, convinced that the play had fallen at the worst possible time, had his eyes riveted on his phone. It was still daytime and he was hoping for some more news.

They arrived at Worcester College at seven in the evening and walked around the great green lawn of its English garden. From a distance, they could glimpse the chestnut tree hanging over the lake which had been the jewel in the college crown for over a hundred years. They picked up the pace. The play was due to start in half an hour. They took their places on the tiered seats by the edge of the lake. A boat floated silently into view, lit by spotlights. A few sailors were rowing towards them. The water began to ripple before a thunderclap startled those spectators unfamiliar with the prologue of *The Tempest*. It ended in a few cries. The boat came aground on the island. Farhad's phone started vibrating just as Prospero appeared on stage, followed by his daughter, Miranda.

Farhad waited until the end of the first act before returning Parvez's call, as he didn't want the screen to glare in the middle of the performance. As soon as he could, he hurried down the path towards the main building so as not to disturb anyone. Still undercover inside the foundation, the grocer had just overheard a conversation: Reza's double-dealing had been found out. The woman in the suit had just directed an Algerian with an Errol Flynn-style moustache into the meeting room where the directors were deciding his fate.

Farhad asked Parvez not to leave Reza's side, and to stay at the foundation until he left.

As soon as the second act got under way, he made an effort to spot Karim on stage. He recognised him from his well-placed baritone voice. He was Ariel, the spirit of the island.

Farhad was having difficulty keeping up with the plot, as his mind kept wandering back to Reza. If he was in danger, then all the information he had leaked must have been true. Either way, the attack on the 7th of May could not be halted. The goods had already been dispatched by cargo. The container would be delivered at the specified time and place. There was no stopping it, and the struggle to seize it would be all the more difficult. They had to prepare themselves. Whichever way he looked at it, he always came to the same conclusions.

By the end of the play, his mind was made up: the case had become too serious not to notify the authorities. He explained the gist of it to Neila as they went up to congratulate Karim. She was shaken. She knew by now just how dear Reza was to him.

Once Karim had been put in the picture, he suggested they contact Ridley, who had close links with the secret services. He persuaded Farhad not to take the last train back to London but to stay so he could speak to the professor in the morning. He would slip a note in his pigeonhole. Karim was talking nineteen to the dozen. His expression was grim, despite his elfin costume and gold stage make-up. He didn't wait for Farhad's answer before calling the Randolph Hotel and booking a double room. He seemed to be going at full pelt whereas Farhad was drained, crushed by the guilt of having put Reza at so much risk.

When they got to the quadrangle, Farhad and Neila wished to cut the evening short. Karim understood completely; he left them under the arches and rejoined the cast for a drink.

That night, Farhad was distant. He wasn't in the mood

for intimacy. Thanks to him, Reza was caught up in an impossible situation. He cursed himself for not being able to help him. He thought through the conversation he would have with Ridley in the morning, in order to ensure it would be as strategic as possible.

The meeting in the college was fixed for nine o'clock in the morning. The early-rising professor had seen Karim's note.

Farhad called Parvez before he reached the imposing college door on Beaumont Street. As there was no answer, he left a message to ensure his friend would go back to the foundation.

'Good morning, my boy,' boomed the professor as soon as he came into the same familiar study. 'I've heard about your work. You've made a good start, haven't you? What brings you here today?'

Farhad explained how, after his workshops, little surveillance cells had been spontaneously set up at the heart of various communities, and described how effective they had turned out to be.

'Thanks to their help, we know that a terrorist attack is being planned and we have managed to contact some of those involved. However, the stakes are too high for us to deal with the situation on our own.'

'You've succeeded in keeping your independence thus far, which is already quite a feat,' said the professor, recalling their conversation in the autumn.

They both realised now that it was too risky to go it alone.

'It is vital I remain on the frontline,' Farhad continued. 'Three terrorists have already agreed to be replaced.'

He described how it would work. Until now, Reza, his childhood friend, had been their informant at the Al-Rhubni Foundation, but now that he had just been uncovered, he was in grave danger. That was one of the reasons why he was asking for assistance.

The professor immediately called an MI5 agent who would discreetly take charge of operations. This was a very different side to him; a new Ridley who gave out sharp orders, confident that they would be obeyed at once.

As soon as he hung up, Ridley had to excuse himself as his first tutorial of the day was about to begin.

Once he had left, Farhad felt slightly better. The meeting had been brief, but he had obtained the protection he was looking for. He quickly checked his messages. He realised that from now on any information from Reza would be false, but he didn't care. He needed the reassurance of hearing his voice. No messages.

He walked back to get Neila, his eyes glued to his phone. As he crossed the road in front of the Ashmolean Museum, he was nearly run down by a student cycling past, but hardly noticed. He carried on changing his phone's SIM card as he walked up the wide steps of the Randolph.

He found Neila absorbed in her lecture notes. When she heard the door open, she turned to him, a worried expression on her face. Her delicate features matched the rose-tinted shades on the toile de Jouy wallpaper in the old-fashioned room. He was touched, and grateful to her for being a source of calm through the turmoil of the last few days.

An hour later they went off to the station hand in hand. Farhad slept throughout the journey, under the anxious gaze of his girlfriend.

She was comforted by his decision to go to the authorities for back-up.

XVIII

Neila and Farhad met Michael Shea on the platform at Paddington. Neila was surprised at how ordinary the secret agent appeared; a far cry from Fleming's hero. Michael was not particularly captivating or eloquent. But he was perceptive. As he drove them in his Renault Espace, he asked few questions and simply nodded as he listened to their replies. He suggested they meet the grocer straight away.

Parvez had just come back from the foundation. He had a distressed look on his face. It was bad news. He had just watched Reza get into a fierce argument with one of his superiors, much to the shock of the accounting department. As the big day approached, they were clearly struggling to keep it together. If it hadn't been for the hope that Reza would lead them to his contacts, he would have been bumped off on the spot.

Michael took some time to convince an apprehensive Farhad not to try to warn Reza, as it could scupper the whole plan. He promised he would take personal responsibility for his friend's safety and would do everything in his power to protect him.

They moved on to discuss the practicalities of the operation.

Was the plot's mastermind already in London? Parvez confirmed that he had overheard snippets of a conversation giving instructions to his driver about his imminent arrival. His address was near a canal, in a London neighbourhood with an Italian name. Michael deduced that it was most likely Little Venice. Parvez added that the Fiat Ducato would be armoured, but the meeting place on the 7th of May was still to be New Haven.

Michael listened carefully as Neila and Parvez described in detail how the three repentant men had been convinced to give up their places. He reminded them that it was imperative that they keep playing the game and continue to accept payment from the foundation to avoid any suspicion.

Farhad had stayed quiet. Many of these details were new to him. He was proud to have chosen his friends so well. Without Michael, he would never have grasped the complexity of their task.

But this was no time for such thoughts. There was still so much to arrange before the seventh. And Reza was risking his life at every moment! He changed his SIM card once again. It would probably be impossible for Reza to communicate with him, particularly as, according to Parvez, he had been under constant surveillance since his supervisors discovered that he had got his hands on top-secret files. They had even considered locking him up. The conspirators all stopped talking as soon as they saw him.

Parvez had watched him in his office, snowed under piles of files from morning until evening. It seemed he was being assigned more and more urgent tasks each day.

All this had begun after the moustachioed Algerian had met with the executives. As he was leaving, Parvez had heard him suggest that they keep their treasurer as occupied as possible so he wouldn't have time to catch his breath. If necessary, they should take him out.

Now Farhad had only one thing in mind: he had to go to the foundation that very morning!

'How can you even think of wrecking the whole plan when hundreds of lives are in danger?' Neila cried, wild with worry. 'If you go, they will know for sure that Reza is not acting alone,' she said, looking him straight in the eye. 'Everything you've been working on for months will be ruined. The attack is only a few hours away. Your job is to be in the van,' she continued, firmly. 'You cannot throw yourself in the lion's mouth and risk leaving Parvez and Karim alone tonight.'

Farhad looked away. He had to admit that she was right. If they delayed the operation, Reza wouldn't be able to provide them with information on the new plan of attack.

The best way to take them down was to let them carry out their plans. But it was hard to control his anguish. The idea of leaving Reza on the frontline until the operation was over caused him great distress.

XIX

That evening, Farhad arrived alone in New Haven at half past six, according to the instructions. Parvez and Karim were to meet him there. The three friends had taken separate means of transportation to get to the port. Karim was coming straight from Oxford.

As they were not supposed to know each other, they had agreed to get into the car in silence.

On their way, not once had any of them wondered how he had got into such a situation. It seemed normal to them to do whatever they could, even pretend to be terrorists, to prevent a massacre. Several scenarios had been envisaged with Michael. They had even rehearsed manoeuvres in his Renault in order to learn how to put men out of action in a confined space.

Farhad arrived first. The white Ducato on the left of the port's parking lot was unlocked. He settled in the middle of the back seat as instructed, set up the camera with ease and waited. After endless minutes, the door slid open and two individuals slipped in beside him, pushing him towards the window. A third man joined them a few seconds later. His two friends arrived in succession.

Not one instant had he doubted they would come.

'The boat has already docked,' said the man on the right, 'but we have to wait.'

The heavy silence that had resumed after this banal sentence was broken by the driver's door opening. The vehicle started and then parked behind the imposing silhouette of a cargo vessel whose rusty mass stood out against the bluish twilight. Then the man on the right ordered Parvez, Farhad and one of the two henchmen to follow him.

The four men waited for the arrival of a container which they had to carry back to the car. Its weight led Farhad to guess that it was probably a bomb sheathed in lead to avoid being detected. He had read that radioactive substances, well isolated, were more than likely to be smuggled in by sea. He broke out in a cold sweat. The four men neared the back of the car and with difficulty pushed the container inside.

'Any detonator could do the job and would create a bloodbath as well as insidiously contaminate the whole city,' Farhad said to himself, hoping that Parvez would be able to defuse it easily. He was gestured to get back into the vehicle. During the whole procedure, he had avoided Parvez's eyes.

Once inside, he realised that it would be hard to neutralise the three men, even though he had with him a syringe of propofol, a powerful anaesthetic, procured by Parvez's son, the medical student.

'If our plan fails,' he thought as they drove on, 'MI5 will step in and eliminate all the passengers in the car, including ourselves. At least other civilians will be saved from a massacre.'

Then his eyes fell on the back of Karim's neck and his heart sank. The courageous soul had embraced his mad plan as soon as he had returned from the Emirates. If they all died in action, their fate would no doubt be linked to that of the terrorists. Was he thinking at this very moment about how disillusioned his father would be? Farhad was convinced MI5 would not report the true story after their death. Why should they bother? And he saw then how little trust he had in the English.

The road from New Haven to Little Venice seemed endless. The three friends stoically waited for the right moment to defuse the bomb and neutralise the others, a task that seemed beyond their capabilities.

They passed a few cars. The headlights lit up their faces, bringing them out of the darkness for a brief instant and blinding Farhad. He did not budge, determined as he was to succeed.

They entered the metropolis at about eight o'clock. It was a clear night. As they streaked by, Farhad saw the neighbourhoods, with their rows of shops and brick houses. Nothing was familiar. He had no points of reference; he couldn't take anything for granted.

They went through Streatham Park, skirted the canal and entered the paved garden of a house. A giant of a man, accompanied by several armed guards, approached.

The three stooges got out. Their greetings were far from reassuring. As they had not been asked to join them, Farhad, Karim and Parvez, mesmerised, watched the scene through the windscreen.

Suddenly, the sliding door opened and the giant plopped heavily into the seat beside Farhad while one of the guards cautiously handed him a large briefcase that he put on his lap. On tenterhooks, Farhad wondered if they were coming too, since the three other men had given up their seats. As of a single mind, Karim and Parvez refrained from turning around.

They drove off, to Farhad's great relief. Only the giant had remained with them in the passenger compartment, and the driver on the other side of the glass partition was paying no attention. Farhad's nerves settled. 'He's the brain,' he told himself. 'That's him!' He realised, while the car sped past the banks of the Thames, that he would not be too difficult to neutralise. It was his turn to act.

Not knowing how much time he had left, Farhad clutched the syringe in his pocket, waiting for the right moment. He wondered, looking at the man's impassive countenance, how he could appear so calm with death around the corner. His mind went back to the fanatics who had made life miserable for so many of his compatriots, recalling his ancestor Nader the Elder, the first to challenge the Grand Master of the Assassins.

By then they had left the Mall and were heading towards Mayfair. He took a minute to review his plan. The Piccadilly lights were already flooding the interior of the Ducato. The immense windows of the Fortnum and Mason department store appeared with their gay decorations. Further along, on the left, the Meridien Hotel was the turning-point into Regent Street… Young couples embracing in front of cinemas, families coming out of the theatres, folk strolling into restaurants… myriads of people paraded under his gaze, an ordinary Saturday that could end in catastrophe.

'Leicester Square!' thought a horrified Farhad. 'That's where they are going to strike, on a busy evening.'

Galvanised by rage, and without giving any indication of his movements to the others, he passed the syringe into his left hand, popped off the cap and, with a rapid movement, stuck it into his neighbour's thigh. The thin needle easily went through the cloth of his pants. The sturdy body hardly twitched; the lightning product had worked. The driver remained imperturbable, aware of nothing.

Farhad was overcome by weariness. But he pulled himself together, the hardest bit was still to come. He grabbed the briefcase and opened it. The electric detonator was ticking. Four minutes and seven seconds were left as the car pulled up at the end of the major thoroughfare. He touched Parvez's shoulder and they stared at each other gravely. He passed him the device in silence.

Karim watched petrified as the engineer's dexterous hands worked slowly and precisely.

It was over. But no time to rejoice. For Farhad had a new battle to fight. Haunted by another imminent risk, he threw a grateful look to his friends as he disappeared down the entrance to the Underground. Michael would shortly be there to sort everything out.

Fahrad had to rush to the foundation.

XX

The Fiat Ducato's mad race had unfortunately ended in Leicester Square, fifteen stops away from the foundation. In the carriage, his ear stuck to his phone, Farhad tried desperately to contact Michael Shea but there was no network underground. His thoughts clouded as he imagined his friend's dismay if the British barged in. He was furious at himself for leaving him in the hands of the terrorists. He was the only one who knew that Reza was held a prisoner by these monsters. How could he prove his innocence if they were all picked up by the police before his arrival? What a sorry fate awaited him.

He felt more and more exhausted. The train was now riding in the open; only two more stops to go… Police sirens could be heard in the distance… Were they moving in on the foundation? How would Reza react to their raid, he who didn't even want them to be alerted?

He rushed out. There was a crowd of people in front of a roadblock. He could hear very English voices shouting. Shots had already been fired. 'The British are already here!' he thought in consternation. Two vans were blocking the street. He cut back, hoping to find a side entrance that would be still open. Rebuffed, he staggered the other way. A police officer, his suspicions raised by his erratic gait, called his colleagues, giving them the description of a man who claimed he knew people inside the building. Farhad tried a last bluff and slowed down his stride, determined to slip through the first block that didn't look as compact. He approached it, mingled with the throng and tried to force his way in, his head spinning with the noise. He was making headway when he was hit with a truncheon and lost consciousness.

When he came back to his senses, Michael told him the news. Reza had thrown himself out of the window as soon as MI5 had moved in.

'Everything points to suicide,' he said.

Farhad was overwhelmed by grief. He still desperately tried to comprehend how Reza had been caught up in this trap.

Nabil was the contact who had drawn him in. In London, he used to fix their meetings in a Battersea pub. He had a slight limp and his hip was painful. Reza had shown his concern and he had listened to the story of the man's fights and battles.

At thirty-seven, the Algerian who sported a moustache from another era, was a master in the art of seduction and possessed the financial means to back it up. He was the recruiter for the foundation, thanks to the well-endowed bank account of a follower of Abu Hamza, the preacher who incited violence from a London mosque. He had entrusted Nabil with the mission before being imprisoned. In the guise of a benefactor, the Algerian who operated between Paris and London, recruited floundering young people and would surf on their bewilderment and their spiritual misery. Over a series of lunches, he would try to probe them. He knew how to adapt his discourse. When he spoke of politics or religion, he could be very convincing.

Nabil had noticed Reza, a well-dressed Iranian, outside the Great Mosque in Paris as he was gazing, enthralled, at the Moorish architecture. After a conversation, he had recognised his capabilities, and had immediately thought of making him the treasurer of the foundation.

After several days and meetings, Nabil realised that Reza's poise and skills would soon lead to his being recruited by a bank, and made him a firm offer for the job in London

At first glance, upon his arrival, Reza had really disliked the capital where a hospital was going to give way to a five-star hotel, but he had come to terms with that. His studio on the edge of Brixton in a low-income area suited him, as anything was better than the ostentation and luxury that was pervading London.

Just as Farhad had done, he had searched around him for distinguished Englishmen, modelled after the myth of the gentleman. Later, overburdened with work, he had stopped looking.

Nabil was a generous employer, and thanks to him, Reza felt he was serving a just cause while earning his living. His numerous 'protégés' were never left unsupported. Until Farhad had opened his eyes, Reza had never suspected his superiors.

As treasurer, he had then noticed that Abu Hamza's followers were incessantly endowing the foundation, clearly stating that they wanted most of the funds to be used to form new cells. As long as the money kept rolling in, enrolment would increase. And Nabil, the only one of his peers to work both in France and in the UK, attracted the best of them to allow the network to function and grow. All the recruits received a stipend that was enough for them to live decently. Giving the bare minimum was a tactic to ensure they would come back to him when in need, which enhanced their loyalty. Moreover, these young recruits, who had no financial concerns, were upheld as role models during the Friday sermons. The foundation excelled in its smoke and mirrors role.

XXI

Farhad blamed himself for failing to protect Reza. He felt responsible for sending his dearest friend to his death, and there was nothing that could console him.

Attempts to shake him out of his despair had been fruitless. Any mention of the operation's success seemed to him to be in particularly poor taste. Only Neila and Karim were wise enough to keep quiet and just hope that time would heal the wound.

To make matters worse, the investigation conducted by Scotland Yard was painting Reza in a very negative light. Their report framed him as one of the leading figures of the foundation and associated him with the recruitments, because all of the payment orders had been signed off by him. Furthermore, the press had smeared him and made him out to be an international terrorist, since they had no other name to target. The most unfavourable reports of his character and connections were being dug up and circulated to every French and British household.

Only MI5 knew the truth about his involvement in the

attack, but they were refusing to divulge it for the time being. 'We have to wait,' Michael Shea kept reiterating. Farhad noticed that past promises were of little concern to him. If he and his friends had had no problems defusing a bomb in a car as it was zooming along at full speed, under the noses of formidable terrorists, why had it been impossible to save Reza? Farhad was bitter. He had put the life of his closest friend into the hands of the British, despite his suspicions that they might be disloyal.

Intuitions are like clouds. We ignore them at our peril, especially when they forebode disaster.

From now on, his aim in life would be to clear Reza's name.

Pari *khanoum*, Reza's mother, had heard the tragic news from a friend, who had rushed to her house to give her an abridged version of the events. This man knew how hurt she had been when after a dispute about religion with his father, Reza had left the house never to return.

After a few days of hesitation, Farhad called her but couldn't find the words to comfort her. She described how furious Reza's father was: his grief at losing his son had been nothing compared to the shame of seeing the press sully their name and drag it through the mud. His anger was hindering his grieving process.

After her insistence, her husband reluctantly agreed to speak to Farhad, who made every effort to convince him that his son was a hero. Even by the end of the conversation, Farhad could hear him muttering about the disgrace and dishonour blackening the family name. He hung up rather abruptly after the usual Iranian pleasantries, which sounded hollow under the circumstances.

When his brother, Reza's uncle, read his nephew's name in the crime section of a newspaper, he kicked himself for not forcing him to come back to France when Farhad had warned him that the foundation might be untrustworthy.

As for Maryam, Farhad's mother, she had got quite a shock when she heard Reza's name mentioned on the radio, as she didn't believe for one minute that her own son wouldn't be implicated in the tragedy in some way. It took him some time to explain to her how heroic Reza had been. By now the story had become like a mantra, though each repetition rubbed more salt into his wound. He couldn't bring himself to go into more detail, but he promised to tell her the whole story when he returned.

As the university year was drawing to a close, Farhad was considering going back to Paris.

The reconciliation with citizens of Muslim descent that he had been advocating over the past year seemed like wishful thinking. He now saw himself as a hybrid, estranged even to himself, torn between East and West. Beneath its welcoming exterior and its respect for other customs, Great Britain had not given him a good impression of his difference. It had categorised him as an Iranian, a moderate, a Shiite Muslim. He could stay in this country for a hundred years without ever fully integrating. Even though on the surface the British considered these differences to be culturally enriching, the country continued to treat their minorities differently. The journey back to Iran had been a key moment for Farhad. Even there he had felt too Westernised to be able to fit in. Someone who could live anywhere and feel at home nowhere; this is what he had become.

The more he thought about it, the more certain he was that France was the only country capable of fulfilling his needs. He had started his education there in primary school and had never felt like a foreigner. Most of his generation had also been at ease and had settled into the republican system. France had never opted for communitarianism, which encouraged the growth of real pockets of immigration. Perhaps the barriers of low-cost social housing around Paris were hardly any better, yet the different communities interacted more and got on quite well with each other, which seemed to suggest that their problems were mainly economic. Certainly, he had heard of teenagers from underprivileged backgrounds complaining about their struggle to integrate, and their elders bemoaning the lack of jobs. In France, he felt able to tackle the situation head on.

As he weighed up the situation, Farhad considered the so far circumscribed scope of his workshops. He had improved maybe a thousand people's views of Islam, and they would spread the word. But before they could hope for a wider awareness, a more methodical approach was needed, perhaps even a real debate about reform. He would no doubt do this in the medium term, but for the moment, he wanted to concentrate on encouraging

Muslims to take responsibility in their own communities and helping them find their place in Western societies.

That was where his fight would be.

Life returned to normal. After a few weeks, it was business as usual. Farhad tried hard to focus on his classes and workshops, committed to pursuing his goals.

Sticking to his intention to clear Reza's name, he wrote a reminder in his notepad to get back into contact with the former head of MI5, the friend of the Dean of the Global Institute for International Affairs he had met when he first arrived in London.

Parvez, who had watched over him with respectful discretion, got on with renewed energy into launching monitoring task forces in new communities.

With the end of the academic year approaching, Neila spent most of her time in Southall when she wasn't revising.

Karim was waiting to defend the doctoral thesis which he had just submitted. As he had a few days to spare, he agreed to go hawking with his father. He tried, in vain, to convince Farhad to join him to take his mind off things. He would have liked so much to show him his home country.

Farhad had other things on his mind, and there was no question that the Dean's friend would know what to do.

When they met, Farhad got straight to the point, describing the charges that were laid against Reza. When he mentioned the notes they had left each other under the stone, the authoritative man sat up and took notice.

'Then the proof of his innocence is in your hands, my boy,' the director exclaimed. 'Have the notes validated by an expert graphologist, and I'll set the record straight.'

Sometimes when you are trapped in your own head, a fresh eye is all you need to show you that the solution is already within reach.

XXII

Karim came back from his trip more galvanised than ever. He was eager to share with Farhad the plans he had made with his father. After the emir had heard about their involvement in foiling the attack, he had stepped up his support. He would be backed by many of his friends and acquaintances who were also outraged by the image that was being projected of their religion.

'We can talk it through properly on Saturday,' said Karim.

'Saturday?' repeated a confused Farhad. 'Oh, yes, the ball! Of course, I had completely forgotten about it.'

Karim was not surprised, and he was simply relieved that Farhad hadn't turned the invite down point-blank. He knew how hard it would be for him to go to a party.

'I've also organised a private viewing of the mineral collection at Christ Church on Saturday. Would you come with me? I don't fancy going by myself, but I have to do it as a favour to my father's friend.'

Farhad winced as he recalled that he had tried several months back to see the vast collection and had been flatly turned down. Since the events of that spring, his plan to get the Alamut stone back had entirely slipped his mind.

How could he have let himself forget something like that? Had he let his emotions swamp him? Was this life's way of giving him a wake-up call?

Neila enthusiastically accepted the invitation to the ball, which somewhat dispelled Farhad's fears about her intentions. He was hoping she would come to Paris with him. He had asked her and was anxiously awaiting her response. They had seen less of each other lately, and it was unsettling him. He cared about her very much but did not wish to press her for a decision.

On the day of the ball, the two friends arrived at Christ Church porter's lodge, which looked out onto the main quadrangle. In the distance, Jean de Bologne's statue of Mercury with winged heels seemed as if it were about to fly off on some far-flung mission.

When they got to the library, Karim gestured to his friend to wait at the door while, out of courtesy, he let the college know that there were two of them. An old man, hunched over with age, hurried over to welcome them. He was long past retirement age, but his beaming face was a testament to the pleasure he derived from having young visitors. He had bent over backwards to keep the job he had held for so many years as curator of the library. Since he was competent and willing to work on a voluntary basis, the university had made accommodations.

He was very knowledgeable and spoke with enthusiasm. He passed his hand over the glass doors of the cabinets as he led them into the room where the most important artefacts were displayed, arranged according to their origin and composition. There was such a variety of shapes, textures and colours that, without his help, they would not have known where to begin.

When the librarian saw them lingering over each display, he offered them a powerful magnifying glass. He also showed them a few particularly dense stones from the Prehistoric era, which he let them handle. The young men could have examined them all day, their heads almost touching as each pointed out different details to the other. Leading them on to the next cabinet, the librarian was touched to see such an unusually eager interaction between his visitors.

'This collection,' he explained, 'is the fruit of the labours of Lord Aspers, the famous geologist. Our exhibition owes so much to his travels, including the rare meteorites he brought back from Persia. I got them from the man himself back in 1964.'

'Oh, look!' cried Karim. 'That's the stone of Alamut. It's the twin of the one my father's friend bought at Sotheby's…'

'So you know this Al-Morabi?'

'Yes, he's the person who asked me to come here. He's my father's friend, and during my last trip, he took us to see the exhibition of his archaeological collection at the Abu Dhabi museum. He told us the whole story of the

Alamut stones, including the one that disappeared and has never been seen again.'

'It's important to note,' intervened the librarian, 'that before he became an infamous murderer, Hassan Sabbah was an enlightened thinker. Philosophers and chroniclers of his time even refer to his early writings as extraordinary. Unfortunately, they were all destroyed by a fire, except the three sentences engraved on the stones.'

'Well, that is the very message I've been asked to report back on.'

'It's in Farsi,' interjected Farhad, picking up the stone.

He fell silent, overwhelmed to finally be holding it in his hands. It was indeed the sister stone of the one he had handled at Sotheby's. Although it was a slightly different shape, it had the same pinkish sparkling incrustations. As he ran his fingers along the inscription, his mind went back to the crypt and the tale of his ancestor, Nader the Elder.

'Well?' Karim encouraged him.

'Ten centuries on, the words are still just as legible as if they had been written yesterday.'

And he passed them his little black notebook, where he had just noted down the translation: 'Under the vault of heaven.'

'It's a shame,' Karim sighed, 'that I can't remember the exact wording on the stone from Abu Dhabi. Something about "existence". According to Al-Morabi, this is the one that was entrusted to Omar Khayyam by the future Master of the Assassins.'

'Wait a minute,' exclaimed the curator. 'That's the opening of one of the poems attributed to Omar Khayyam! I'll go and fetch it.'

He came back with the anthology and read:

Under the star vault,
There can be no existence
Which between good and evil
Ignores the difference.

'That's the gist of Hassan Sabbah's early philosophy in a nutshell,' declared the curator. 'He believed that all men were born with an innate awareness of good and evil. In other words, they have an innate natural empathy before they are taught any morals.'

'That's what the Persians believed,' added Karim. 'The best moral compass is the one inside us. And Kant puts it very well when he talks about the correlation between the stars above our heads and the moral code within us. This correlation is implicit in all sacred texts; it's universal.'

'If we follow this line of reasoning, mankind doesn't need religion to live an ethical life, as we have our innate conscience,' Farhad continued. 'But when they are properly understood, all religions should teach us how to let our actions be guided by the moral compass within us.'

Pleased to see such an in-depth discussion, the curator picked up the stone and started playing with it to give him something to do with his hands. This scholarly man loved sharing his knowledge, but he hated nothing more than being the centre of attention. This was why he had chosen to be the college librarian for fifty-four years.

Once they had thanked him, the two young men shot off down the stairs and back into the sun.

'Sorry for keeping you in that dark room when we could have been punting out in the sun,' said Karim.

'Don't be,' Farhad answered. 'Actually, I found the visit very enlightening. And so unsettling, you have no idea! You won't believe this, but the third stone of Alamut belongs to my family. My ancestor was one of the close Nishapur circle of friends it was intended for. When I went to Iran, I found out that it had always been kept in the crypt of my family home in Isfahan. But then it disappeared, which is why I came to London.'

'I can't believe it… What a history your family has! Your modesty does you credit…'

'That message was in my ancestor's memoirs, and it always guided his life choices,' Farhad said.

'Well yes, what do you think of the message? It's not like Hassan Sabbah stayed particularly true to his principles, is it?' Karim asked.

'That's where his ambiguity lies. He went against what he had sworn to do in his youth. You have to wonder how he changed so dramatically. My ancestor and his descendants did everything they could to fight him. But we can talk about this some other time. Neila will be here soon, and I can't wait to see her.'

It was nearly time for the ball. They met Neila on the high street. Farhad caught sight of her deep, fiery hair from a distance. He put his arms around her and rested his chin on her shoulder. They stayed like this for a few minutes in the golden late-afternoon sun, staring into the distance together.

That evening, Karim came by their hotel to pick them up. He had a drink with Farhad at the bar while they waited for Neila. When they saw her coming down the main stairs, her lilac silk chiffon dress light as air, she took their breath away. 'She's Yeats's "Athena Nike with a natural and unsystematic beauty",' Karim muttered in Farhad's ear.

She smiled at their surprised expressions and took both of their arms as they left, to avoid any praise.

Early on in the evening, Farhad bumped into Ridley in the quad where a Schubert quintet was being performed. 'Reza's name will soon be cleared,' he declared triumphantly, hoping to please Farhad. 'An intervention from on high,' he explained. 'All the same, you have to admit that your friend was playing with fire,' he added as he walked off. Farhad maintained a deadpan expression as he clenched his fists. The English definitely had a lot to learn.

He was unsettled by this news, although it was what he had been working towards. In order to come to terms with it in private, he slipped away to the only spot in the college that had not been taken over by the ball; the rose garden not far from the orchard. There he stayed, hidden from sight, aware that a chapter of his life was coming to an end. Neila and Karim were on the dance floor, revelling in the end of their studies while respecting the fact that he needed some space.

When the air turned colder, he found them in good company, having dinner in a marquee. Neila had cheerfully saved a spot for him beside her, and Karim was careful to steer the conversation towards topics that would include him so that he could get on easily with his friends.

Afterwards, Farhad spoke to Neila. He knew that following him to Paris was asking a lot from her, and he was ready to let her go if that was what she wanted. She kept silent. He glanced at her and thought he might have detected a smile in the twilight. Then she slipped her hand into his, and his heart began to beat madly with hope. His happiness rested on those lips, which sketched a shy smile. He waited without daring to believe it. Neila spoke sincerely in her deep, lilting voice. She had applied for a Master's at Sciences Po, with a good chance of getting a place. The classes would be in English.

Farhad took her slim, willowy figure in his arms, and kissed her passionately, whispering tender words into her ear.

On their way back to the hotel, Farhad's heart was filled with joy. With Neila by his side, there was nothing he couldn't achieve.

EPILOGUE

The Eurostar was practically empty. It was a hot midday at the beginning of July. On leaving the apartment in Montague Place, Farhad had paid a visit to Mrs Holland and somewhat regretfully, for the last time, dawdled in Bloomsbury. And yet he wanted to avoid replaying all the important episodes of that year in his head. He knew that he had at least two months before taking up a permanent job probably in a large company. He felt uneasy about it and tried to analyse his overwhelming angst. That was it: he was afraid of no longer being himself again, caught up in the system. He was comforted by the idea that Neila would soon join him and they would carry on with their philanthropic activities in France.

There was an announcement that the bar was closing in ten minutes, so happily his journey was coming to an end. For the first time he looked out of the windows and saw the outskirts of Paris. 'How odd to have spent a year without coming back despite the capital's proximity.' His thoughts turned to his mother whom he was about to see again. She had insisted on coming to meet him at the station and he had not dissuaded her... He had always initiated their phone conversations. He was grateful that she had accepted his stay in London without any reproach. She had respected his longing for solitude. He got up and took his bag so as to be the first passenger to alight. As soon as the train came to a halt, he saw her waiting on the platform: tall, dark-haired, still beautiful in an impeccable *tailleur* despite the heat, she followed the carriage as he had given her its number. Just as when he was a child and she came to collect him after his skiing holidays, he thought, half-amused, half-annoyed. Then he pulled himself together. Why spoil this pleasure for both of them? Ever since Reza's death, he had come to understand the degree to which those moments were rare and precious.

He got off the train with a warm smile on his face. She held him closely, pretending not to see the changes in her son, his slightly sombre expression and his hollow features. He was simply more serious. It was only natural that he had matured.

She seized his heavy suitcase on wheels and turned towards the parking area, chatting happily away.

'Your suitcase weighs a ton, probably full of books!'

She soon realised she was talking to herself. She sensed her son was fairly exhausted and reduced her chatter. Bouts of silence had never disturbed neither one nor the other.

Maryam took the rue de Richelieu, going towards the Louvre. She wanted to give him a surprise and take him directly to the two-roomed apartment she had rented temporarily in the rue Monge. At least, he could stay for a time in the student area he was fond of… She had understood that too brutal a change would be fatal to her plans. Most likely, he would cross the Seine soon enough and settle on the right bank, the business centre.

Farhad looked at her with an amused smile on his face. She seemed younger than he remembered, and he listened to her talking as to some agreeable tune, not paying attention to each distinct word. He then noticed she spoke his name followed by the qualifier 'joon', meaning 'darling'. He could only see her in profile. But her features had suddenly softened and her stiffness had disappeared.

Not wanting to break the harmony of these moments, Farhad hesitated to raise the issue of the passing away in April of his great-aunt. He felt bad that he had not been able to attend her funeral.

He reproached himself aloud as he usually did when he was troubled for having erased the event from his thoughts. Maryam reassured him. Nobody in the family, not even her daughters, had thought any the worse of him for it.

The car was stuck in a traffic jam and ground to a halt. Maryam turned on the news. Another terrorist plot in London had been averted. The role of a young Iranian had been central in foiling the attack. Farhad sighed. Reza would be cleared. Ridley had kept his promise.

'You cannot imagine how many times I have attempted to re-establish the truth… I spoke to so many friends mostly in vain!'

When he didn't reply, she left him lost in his thoughts for a time. And then, she brought up the link with her current work.

'In the department for diversity at the Commission, we aim to minimise the repercussions of terrorist crimes on the entire Muslim population, and we have come to the conclusion that for a start, more Muslims should be encouraged to speak up and condemn them high and loud. "*The world will not be destroyed by those who do evil, but by those who watch them without doing anything.*" It's Albert Einstein who wrote this.'

'In that sense, Reza will perhaps inspire others…' said Farhad. 'I am glad he has been vindicated,' he sighed.

'As sad as this story is,' his mother added, 'Reza acted virtuously. All of the young must play their part. We haven't left our countries, abandoned our closest relatives and renounced our lives to now witness as silent bystanders the spread of fundamentalism here.'

To change the subject, Farhad asked how his great-aunt Nasrine had been during the last days of her life. 'She was as brave at the end as she ever was,' she added. 'Her last thoughts were for you. In fact, she left a sealed letter and a small memento which the notary has sent to your new address. I have no idea what it is.'

Maryam fell silent. Farhad perked up like a child who hears about a present waiting for him. He was impatient to arrive. The rue Monge was in view. Its buildings followed the curve of the road and he could admire their sunny facades and long running balconies. The street was animated with its terraced coffee shops, bookshops and florists. They parked on a nearby square. Maryam pretended to have an errand to run in the neighbourhood so he could go inside alone. He promised to dine with her that evening.

He dropped his suitcases in the entrance, not even taking his jacket off or looking around. He found the small parcel and the sealed letter on the living room table. It was a short note in which his great-aunt had gone straight to the point.

Farhad joon, don't be sad. I have had a life full of joys and surprises and all of you have meant a lot to me. Watching you grow up, I hoped one day to be able to confide in you the 'mission of memory' and that is done. I entrust you with this object for our descendents. It had never left the crypt. I took it on me to remove it when the revolution occurred. Was I right? I think so. If I did not give it to you before now, it was because you did not need it to succeed. You see, I knew what you were made of. It will be useful if ever your determination fails you.

Whatever you undertake, stay humble and keep your discretion in all circumstances, the proof of true grandeur of the soul, and a tradition in our family. Nowadays, only attention-seekers are valued. It is as well to remind ourselves that fortitude and courage reside in each individual and one must nurture these qualities within oneself before hoping to find them in others. You have that vital force. Wherever you go, you will move mountains.

Farhad's mind was flooded with recent images. No, it was not the memoirs or even this very stone that had brought him back to Tehran, Isfahan and then to London…

He had taken this path, pushed by a force beyond himself. For the first time this year, he had felt the intensity of true life, the joy of having found what would motivate his existence. That strength was now within him and he promised himself never to doubt it.

Farhad squeezed the parcel without opening it and gently placed it on the table. He then rushed down the stairs. He would not need an amulet to give meaning to his life. Once in the street, he looked up at the sky, knowing he would find no reply there. He realised he could from now on be confident and at ease in all cultures. He felt alive and ready to accomplish great deeds.

He gave thanks to his ancestor who, in less than a year, had unleashed his inner strength and given him this ultimate lesson.